"I'm going to be a father?"

"Yes," Cricket said softly. "To triplets, actually."

Jack Morgan couldn't move, couldn't speak. Never had his life rushed by so fast, not even the eight seconds he rode to the buzzer.

This was different.

His brothers congratulated him, pounded him on the back, shook his hand.

He tried to say he was excited, too, but all that came out of his mouth was a rusty croak no one heard over all the sudden hugging and kissing of Cricket.

He knew he needed to say something to her, act pleased, brag like an expectant father—but all he could do was try to keep his knees from knocking together and suck air into his lungs.

He'd never been so scared.

How could *he*—a man who spent all his time on the rodeo circuit—be a father?

Dear Reader,

March is a month for new beginnings—a time when everything feels fresh and new as winter begins to ebb away. Though it's still cold in many places, we can begin making our summer reading lists, as it won't be too much longer before the kids are out of school!

It's time for some healing and new beginnings in the Morgan family. In *The Triplets' Rodeo Man*, Jack Morgan, the eldest son, must find his way back home. But can a wild man like Jack fall for a good girl—the town deacon, no less!—like Cricket Jasper? This is one relationship maybe even stalwart matchmaker/patriarch Josiah Morgan couldn't have bet on—and yet Cricket's long had her eyes on Jack. Used to rodeo life and being the outcast of his family, Jack will have many new challenges if he wants to win Cricket. Is it possible that the ladylike deacon has an even wilder side than his own?

Jack knows his brothers were lured into ready-made family life, in *Texas Lullaby* (June '08), *The Texas Ranger's Twins* (January '09), and *The Secret Agent's Surprises* (February '09), so he's well aware that he's the last bachelor Morgan brother— and the man who has the most to lose. Or gain. Can this black sheep turn into a family man?

I hope you've enjoyed THE MORGAN MEN miniseries. As March brings us hope of reborn wonder in the world around us, I hope you'll let the Morgans and their triumphs over their personal trials warm your corner of the world.

Best wishes and much love,

Tina Leonard

Tina Leonard
THE TRIPLETS' RODEO MAN

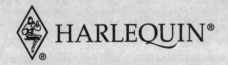

TORONTO • NEW YORK • LONDON
AMSTERDAM • PARIS • SYDNEY • HAMBURG
STOCKHOLM • ATHENS • TOKYO • MILAN • MADRID
PRAGUE • WARSAW • BUDAPEST • AUCKLAND

Recycling programs
for this product may
not exist in your area.

ISBN-13: 978-0-373-75254-6
ISBN-10:   0-373-75254-7

THE TRIPLETS' RODEO MAN

Copyright © 2009 by Tina Leonard.

www.eHarlequin.com

Printed in U.S.A.

ABOUT THE AUTHOR

Tina Leonard is a bestselling author of more than forty projects, including a popular thirteen-book miniseries for Harlequin American Romance. Her books have made the Waldenbooks, Ingram's and Nielsen Book-Scan bestseller lists. Tina feels she has been blessed with a fertile imagination and quick typing skills, excellent editors and a family who loves her career. Born on a military base, she lived in many states before eventually marrying the boy who did her crayon printing for her in the first grade. Tina believes happy endings are a wonderful part of a good life. You can visit her at www.tinaleonard.com.

Books by Tina Leonard

HARLEQUIN AMERICAN ROMANCE

  981—LAREDO'S SASSY SWEETHEART†
  986—RANGER'S WILD WOMAN†
  989—TEX TIMES TEN†
1018—FANNIN'S FLAME†
1037—NAVARRO OR NOT†
1045—CATCHING CALHOUN†
1053—ARCHER'S ANGELS†
1069—BELONGING TO BANDERA†
1083—CROCKETT'S SEDUCTION†
1107—LAST'S TEMPTATION†
1113—MASON'S MARRIAGE†
1129—MY BABY, MY BRIDE*
1137—THE CHRISTMAS TWINS*
1153—HER SECRET SONS*
1213—TEXAS LULLABY**
1241—THE TEXAS RANGER'S TWINS**
1246—THE SECRET AGENT'S SURPRISES**

†Cowboys by the Dozen
*The Tulips Saloon
**The Morgan Men

Many thanks to my editor, Kathleen Scheibling,
for believing in this series, and to
Lisa, Dean and Tim, who understand that
time with family is my personal dream.

A word of gratitude to Pat Wood for assisting me
with this book during a time of her own difficulty—
Pat, you are a true friend.

Any factual errors are mine.

Chapter One

"You reap what you sow."
—Josiah Morgan to his four sons, a general reminder.
Late March, Union Junction, Texas

Jack Morgan stood at his father's bedside in the Union Junction hospital, staring down at the large sleeping man. Josiah Morgan had the power to impress even in his peaceful state. Jack couldn't believe the old lion was ill. He didn't think Pop had ever had so much as a cold in his life.

But if his brother Pete said Pop was weak and in need of a kidney transplant, then those were the facts. Jack took no joy in his father's situation, even though the two of them had never been close. He hadn't seen Pop in more than ten years, not since the night of his rodeo accident, his brothers' car accident and the all-out battle he and Pop had waged against each other.

It had been a terrible night, and the details of it were still etched in his mind. And then there was the letter he'd received through Pete from his father just last month.

Jack, I tried to be a good father. I tried to save you from yourself. In the end, I realized you are too different from me. But I've always been proud of my firstborn son.
Pop

As patriarchal letters went, it stank. Jack figured Pop wouldn't have sent a letter at all if he wasn't sick, so he'd decided to come see for himself. He hadn't expected to care what happened to the miserly old man; Josiah was miserly with his affection, miserly with his money, time, everything. At least that was the father Jack remembered. Still, Jack preferred his father fighting.

"All right, Pop, you old jackass," Jack said, "you can lie in that bed or you can fight."

One eye in the craggy, lined face opened to stare at him as he spoke, then the other opened in disbelief. "Jack," Josiah murmured.

A thousand emotions tore through Jack. "Get up out of that bed, old man."

"I can't. Not today. Maybe tomorrow," Josiah said gamely.

"Damn right," Jack said. "Because if I'm giving you one of my kidneys, I expect you to be jumping around like a lively young pup."

Josiah squinted at him. "Kidney?"

"Hell, yeah," Jack said. "You and I might as well be tied together for a few more years of agony—don't you think? It could be the one thing we have in common. We're apparently the perfect match for a kidney swap, which I find amusing in a strange sort of way. Not any of my brothers—me, the perfect donor match for you. It's almost Shakespearean."

His father shook his head and closed his eyes. "I don't want any favors, thanks."

Jack pulled a chair close to the bed and sat. "No one's trying to do you a favor, you old jackass, least of all me. Quit feeling sorry for yourself, because I sure as hell don't."

Josiah's eyes snapped open, sparks of fire shooting at his son. "No one has ever felt sorry for Josiah Morgan."

Jack nodded. "Glad we got that settled. You'll need to be in the right frame of mind to get healthy for all those brats you thought you needed."

"Brats?"

"You've been bringing children into the family faster than popcorn popping. Pretty selfish of you to drag all those kids in here and then send up the white flag of surrender, don't you think, Pop?"

"I didn't ask to have rank kidneys!" Josiah barked.

Jack stretched his legs out in front of him, legs that had seen a few sprains and breaks from bulls that had taken their own rage out on him. "We all make our choices."

"I did not choose this."

"You've been 'self-medicating' for years. It's one of

the reasons I don't touch a drop of liquor. I decided long ago not to live by your example."

"Alcohol didn't give me kidney disease." Josiah pulled a whiskey bottle from under the sheet and took a swallow he would have deemed "just a drop."

"Sure didn't help it, either." Jack stared at his father. "Pitiful, if you ask me."

"Well, I didn't ask," Josiah snapped, secreting the bottle again.

"It's nice to be able to tell you exactly what I think while you lie there captive. I've waited years for this moment."

Josiah looked at his son. "I guess you think paybacks are hell."

"I guess so, Pop." Jack wasn't about to give his father an inch of sympathy. The old man was mean as a snake. All the charity and benevolence he'd been throwing around in the past few years didn't fool Jack. Josiah Morgan didn't do anything without a motive.

Josiah shook his head. "So many years passed, and you didn't even let me know you were all right. You chased the one thing you cared about all your life—rodeo—and at thirty-two, you decide you're going to give up the one thing that matters to you? You can't ride with one kidney. It'd be foolish."

"I'll take the risks I want, Pop." Jack stood, staring down at his father. He didn't like the old man, would never forgive him for the harsh words over the years. Wouldn't forgive him for never being proud of him. Wouldn't forgive him for blaming him for the car accident his brothers had been in the night Jack had been carted off to the hospital. "It's just a kidney, Pop, and I'm not doing it for you. I'm doing it for my brothers, who are bringing up the families you've saddled them with. You ought to live to reap what you've sown."

"I'm proud of what I've sown!" Josiah shouted after him as he departed. Jack kept walking. It was a kidney he was giving up, not rodeo. Pop had that all wrong.

CRICKET JASPER SPOTTED the lean cowboy loping through the hospital exit and knew immediately who it was. There was no one like Jack Morgan, not in looks nor in sheer magnetism as far as Cricket was concerned. Why he was at the Union Junction Hospital she couldn't guess—he'd had very little contact with his family for years. She'd only met him a time or two in the past couple of months, and that had been purely by chance.

The brief meetings were enough to make her pray to see him again. Oh, yes, as a deacon, Cricket was fond of prayer, and she also knew that the Lord didn't always grant a person what they wanted, particularly if it wasn't in the mortal's best interests. However, she was drawn to Jack from some deep, emotional part of her soul, and she knew this could be her only opportunity for months—if ever again—to catch him. "Jack!" she called, waving.

He hesitated, glanced her way, considered, she knew, retreating in a different direction. She didn't take this personally—Cricket knew retreat was the cowboy's standard reaction when confronted with anyone connected to his family. She caught up to him. "Jack Morgan, it's good to see you."

He looked at her, his gaze skimming over her white dress. "You, too."

She smiled. "You weren't visiting Josiah, were you?" She wanted so badly to allow her eyes to do their own one-stop shopping up and down Jack's loose-hipped body, but she resisted the urge, telling herself to be patient. The hunted never wanted to feel caught, after all, and she was determined to catch Jack Morgan, even if all she got from him was a kiss.

Jack shrugged. "I wouldn't call it a visit."

"Oh, I'm sure that meant the world to him." Cricket gave him her most friendly, innocent smile. "Now all you need to truly make his day is to find a wife and kids."

He shook his head, not appreciating the joke. Josiah had managed to wrangle three of his four sons to the altar with the promise of a million dollars each, delivering Josiah the grandchildren he wanted in his golden years.

"It won't happen to me," Jack stated. "I'm giving him a kidney, not another branch for the family tree."

Cricket gasped. "A kidney!"

He shrugged. "I keep thinking I'll come to my senses and talk myself out of it, but it hasn't happened yet."

She couldn't catch her breath. It was a stunning revelation for the man who'd vowed to never even visit his father or speak to him again. "Jack, that's…wonderful."

His face was impassive. "Glad you think so."

It was clear he wanted to move on, but Cricket wanted to keep him right where he was. "When's the surgery?"

"Don't know. I need to talk to the doctor about the details. Pop says he doesn't want my kidney, but Pop doesn't always get what he wants. I can wait him out on this one."

Her eyes went wide. "No one told me."

"Maybe we don't need prayer, Deacon," Jack said.

"I'll be praying anyway, cowboy," she shot back.

They stared at one another silently, each making their own private assessment. A hundred thoughts ran through Cricket's mind. Why was he doing this? *Forgiveness. Redemption.* What Jack would never admit about himself—he loved his father, and his family mattered to him.

"You're a good man, Jack," she murmured.

"Don't kid yourself, Deacon." And with that, he walked away.

She watched him go. If he was aware that she had a crush on him, he ignored it steadfastly. She doubted he thought much about her at all. What did he know about her, other than that she was friends with Suzy, Priscilla and Laura, women who had married his brothers. There would never be anything between them. Like roping wind, she didn't have a chance of capturing Jack Morgan.

But she still felt an undeniable pull toward him, feelings that defied her normally practical heart.

This would take some thought. Josiah hadn't bothered to match make for this son because he was unmatchable. Gabe had been fixed up with Laura Adams, who had a young son and daughter. Gabe had fallen like a tree. Dane had been determined not to repeat Gabe's surrender to his father's wishes, but Suzy Winterstone had been moved into the Morgan ranch as a housekeeper, bringing with her little twin girls. Spellbound, Dane had followed his brother to the altar. Pete had wanted to give up the military for a life closer to home but never planned to marry, and certainly not the woman he called Miss Manners, Priscilla Perkins. His father had found quadruplet orphans who needed parents and persuaded Priscilla and Pete to marry. Josiah had nearly completed his family tree, and now Jack was willing to extend the old man's life, giving him the time he needed.

Jack had better watch out. Josiah lived to build his family, and while Jack might give up a kidney, he also might find himself giving up his freedom. Cricket frowned. She knew Josiah too well. As soon as he could draw a healthy breath—and maybe even before—the man would start hunting a bride for Jack. Oh, Josiah would be very sneaky, very underhanded, but before he knew it, Jack would be roped and tied to the Morgan ranch, no matter how much he thought it couldn't happen to him.

The problem as Cricket saw it was that Josiah had always chosen women with children for his sons, and Cricket had none. Nor could she simply seduce Jack into her bed and catch him that way. Not that she would, though the seduction part was worth investigating because she had a feeling it would be a heavenly experience. As a deacon, she'd look mighty fallen to her congregation if she came up pregnant and unmarried.

Cricket mulled over her other options. There were

none, as far as she could see. Walking into Josiah's hospital room, she found him surrounded by cute, young nurses. Josiah appeared pleased to have this beautiful companionship. It was public knowledge that the wealthy man had one son who was still single, and there were certainly plenty of willing bridal candidates making themselves known to Josiah. She had to make certain he didn't get that baby-making glow in his eyes for Jack. "Hello, Josiah," she said, bending down to give him a kiss on the forehead.

The nurses left the room one by one. Josiah grinned at Cricket. "What did you bring me?" he demanded.

"Cookies," she said.

"Good girl."

"I saw Jack as I was coming in."

Josiah nodded, pleased. "I always knew he'd come around."

The fact was, no one had ever thought Jack would come around—there wasn't a gambler in the county who would have taken a wager on it. Cricket smiled. "Did you?"

"No." Josiah smiled. "Just felt like bragging for a minute."

"You're entitled," Cricket said. "So I hear you might get a new kidney."

"That's what he says," Josiah said. "But I have no intention of taking his kidney."

"Why not?"

"Because he'll still ride rodeo." Josiah eased himself up on his pillow. "He just wants to make me crazy. It's his favorite thing to do, payback for the years he thinks I was a bad parent."

She looked at the elderly gentleman. "The story I heard was that rodeo was in Jack's blood. Nothing anyone can do about that."

"True," Josiah said. "but he can't ride with one kidney."

"But you know he would and that would make you crazy."

"Right." Josiah nodded. "I don't mind heading off into the wild blue yonder, but I do mind sitting around worrying like a durn fool about my durn stubborn son."

"You have a lot to live for."

"Oh, hell. You're a religious person, Cricket. You're supposed to spout that kind of nonsense. A man lives to *do*."

"So?" Cricket demanded. "What's your point?"

"My point is that I'm not taking Jack's kidney just so I can spend a few more years on this earth!" Josiah bellowed. "What good would it do me if he got bucked off and stomped? Do you know how often cowboys get stomped?"

"Perhaps some protective gear—"

"Bah!" Josiah tossed off his covers impatiently. "Have them turn down the heat in here, Cricket. It's nearly April. Why do they have the heat so high? I'm not some sissy old man who can't make my own body heat! By heaven, I'm not a corpse yet."

She smiled. "It is a bit warm in here."

"Hey, Deacon," Josiah said. "Sneak me out of this joint."

Her eyes went wide. "I can't do that. Why didn't you ask Jack to? He's the rebel, isn't he?"

"Oh, he wouldn't do it. He's Mr. Giving-My-Kidney-to-Make-Pop-Feel-Guilty." Josiah sniffed, obviously upset.

"Josiah," Cricket said, "we'd all like to see you gracing the earth awhile longer."

"Oh?" His brows beetled, white and thick on his strong forehead. "Who are *we?*"

"Me, for one."

"Well, that's one."

"Okay," Cricket said. "What would make you feel like you have a reason to live? An important enough mission to keep your boots planted firmly on the earth, so that you can be a gracious recipient of the gift your son is trying to give you?"

He glowered at her. "I'll tell you, Deacon," Josiah said. "Find a good woman with children who needs a husband and somehow convince her and Jack to get hitched. That would be worth hanging around to see."

Cricket swallowed. "A woman with children?"

He nodded. "There's no reason to leave young children without a father when we have plenty of resources in the Morgan family. If you have a magic wand, wave it and make it snappy, say, in the next twenty-four hours, before they bring in that infernal kidney I'm getting. Grandchildren are what old horses like me live to see."

"Josiah," Cricket said faintly, "you're asking for a miracle, not a magic wand."

"Don't you do miracles? Isn't that your thing?"

She paused. "Certainly I believe in them, but Jack hasn't been…I mean, I know nothing of his personal life. He could already have a girlfriend."

"That would make your job easy."

"If she had children already," Cricket reminded him. "Just getting him to the altar would be incredibly difficult, but fixing him up with a single mother who would suit him is likely beyond impossible." Cricket tried to ignore her own racing heartbeat. There was no way she could honestly match make for Jack Morgan—not with the way her heart jumped every time she saw him. Ever since January, when she'd seen him in the bull-riding ring at the rodeo, she'd known she had the man in her sights who could undo everything rational she thought about men and marriage. A rodeo cowboy could never be the perfect man for her, and yet, her heart was drawn to the devil-may-care in him. "I can't do it, Josiah. It's not my place to do so."

"Hell's bells," Josiah complained. "A family would settle my son down, and that would be best for everyone."

"What if he met a woman he fell in love with and then made a family? Wouldn't that be better?"

"No," Josiah said stubbornly. "Because Jack will never marry unless he has to. It's kind of like visiting his old man—it's costing him a kidney. Whatever woman catches him is going to have to rope, drag and throw my son to the altar, and he'll yowl like he's trussed on a Fourth of July grill."

That was probably prescient. And she didn't want Jack "yowling" if she was the one tying him down— what woman wanted to catch her man that way? "I'll just finish the drapes for your house that you've been wanting, which Suzy and Priscilla and I promised you months ago. How about that? Wouldn't new drapes give you a reason to come home healthy?"

He shook his head. "That's the dumbest thing I've ever heard. You are no good at negotiating, Cricket Jasper, particularly as I know you have a thing for my son. However, you'll never catch him if you're planning on wrapping yourself in drapes like Scarlett O'Hara, my girl. No, to catch Jack, you'll have to be willing to lay body and soul on the line. He's not exactly the curtains type, more like cots and coyotes, if you get my drift."

Cricket did, indeed, get Josiah's drift, and considered herself well warned.

Chapter Two

Jack hesitated outside his father's door, realizing he was the topic of conversation between the pretty deacon and his father. He heard his father sneakily trying to get Cricket to romance him; he heard Cricket backing away from the idea and offering up her services as Martha Stewart instead. Part of Jack wanted to snicker at his father's failed attempt at matchmaking, the other part of him was seriously annoyed Pop couldn't just give the whole family-expansion thing a rest. But that was typical of the old man. He couldn't be happy knowing he had a chance to get well. It had to be the family and kids and happily-ever-after for Pop—as if Jack and his brother's had ever had that for one single day in their lives.

Thankfully, the good deacon was too angelic for Jack—and too crafty for Pop. Still, it shocked him that Pop thought the deacon had the hots for him. Then again, Pop was entitled to a delusion or two.

"Josiah, I'll play cards with you, but only if you quit sipping out of that bottle," Jack heard Cricket say.

"Because if you don't quit, you'll be too relaxed to tell Jack that you don't want his silly old kidney."

Jack leaned close to the door, amused by Cricket's coddling.

"I hadn't thought of that," Josiah said.

"And the liquor will skew the blood tests," Cricket said practically. "It will mess up your medication, and the next thing you know, you'll be at Jack's mercy."

"You have a point." There was silence for a long while. "I do not want to be at anyone's mercy."

"Of course you don't. Who does?"

"Not me, durn it. Toss this bottle into your purse and take it home to the ranch for me, would you? Store it in my liquor cabinet."

"I will. It'll be waiting safe and sound for your return."

"And when will that be? C'mon, Deacon, I want you to spring me from this place."

"Aren't you happy here? You seem to be getting plenty of attention from the ladies," Cricket said, her tone soothing.

"My heart is already taken," Josiah said. "Anyway, I was hunting for a girl for Jack."

"When I saw him ride in January, there was a rumor going around that your son has all the female attention he wants," Cricket said. "Let's just focus on you."

"Was he any good at rodeo?" Josiah asked. "I've never seen him ride."

"He was average," Cricket said.

Jack straightened. Average! That day he'd placed first with his highest score, the best ride he'd ever had.

"Oh," Josiah said. "I was kind of hoping he was good at the one thing he's chased all his life."

"Well," Cricket said, "some men are late bloomers."

Jack blinked. The woman was crazy! She didn't know what she was talking about. He hadn't been a late bloomer at anything.

"Later on, Jack mentioned he was considering giving up rodeo," Cricket said, her tone serene. "Let me see…what did he say he going to do?" Jack strained, listening to the deacon spin her incredible yarn.

"Oh," Cricket said, "I remember. He said he'd decided to go into ranching. And do a little math tutoring at the high school. Did you know he got a college degree by correspondence course?"

"He did?" Josiah demanded.

I did? Jack mouthed.

"Yes," Cricket said. "From what I could tell, he's very smart and a huge believer in education."

"That makes me very happy," Josiah said. "I wish I'd known all this so that I could have told him how proud I am when he was visiting me. I didn't have a chance," he said sadly. "We always seem to get into a fight right off the bat."

"Oh," Cricket said, "Fathers and eldest sons do that."

"They do?" Josiah said.

"Sure. And eldest daughters sometimes scrabble with their mothers. I argued a time or two with mine. And my brother." Jack heard cards being shuffled. "Anyway, you can tell him how proud you are tomorrow."

"Yes," Josiah said, sounding happy. "I can. And you know, if he really wants to go into ranching, his brothers have started a new breeding business between them. They'd probably really appreciate the help. Heavens knows I've got the land. In fact," he said, lowering his voice so that Jack had to really bend an ear to hear, "it's time for me to rewrite my will."

"Oh, dear," Cricket said, "let's play Twenty-one and not think about wills, Josiah."

"Are preachers supposed to know how to play cards?" Josiah demanded.

"It's either this or dice. Pick your poison, sir." Jack heard the sound of cards being slapped down on a table.

"I'm going to have to divide up the ranch, you know," Josiah said. "Last month I realized I was going to have to leave Jack out. But maybe I've just misunderstood him."

"Most likely," Cricket said.

Jack frowned. Why was the deacon cozying up to his father on his behalf? She wasn't very honest for a cleric—she was a pretty face who told outrageous fibs. Too bad she was such a storytelling wench; she'd almost had him believing all that sweetness she was peddling. Almost. But now he knew Cricket was a woman who would say anything to get what she wanted.

He wasn't sure what Cricket wanted, but he'd know soon enough. Everybody had a price. Except him, of course.

She came out the door suddenly and squashed his toe

on purpose. "That's what you get for eavesdropping," she whispered. "You're going to have to think fast to keep up with your old man, cowboy. Let's see if you can do that, okay?"

Then she popped him on the arm like he was no more than a baseball-playing buddy, tossed her enormous handbag over her shoulder—Pop could have fit a case of whiskey in that thing—and headed off, looking remarkably like a tall, but still cute Audrey Hepburn.

Jack stared after her. That was one pain-in-the-well-worn-butt woman. And unfortunately, she had the asset Jack most appreciated on a female—a very sassy derriere.

Somehow that was even more annoying.

Josiah left the hospital that night. Jack wasn't really surprised when he got the call. He would have done the same. Jack figured if anybody was like him, it was the old man. Pop wasn't going to be a burden, and like his sons, he knew how to hit the escape hatch.

It was up to him to fetch his father. This wouldn't be the easiest thing in the world because Pop didn't want his life extended by taking something from Jack. Pop would consider this gesture sacrilegious, wasteful and downright wrong.

He couldn't blame his father. Since they hadn't spoken in over ten years, Josiah had every right to his feelings. It was bad luck that only Jack was the perfect donor match, which he'd found out after being tested—something he did only after Laura, Gabe's nurse wife, left a message for him at a local rodeo that they were running out of options with Pop. It had been a warning, not a solicitation for help. Still, Jack had felt a curiosity and an obligation to find out if he was an eligible donor. Quietly, he'd had the testing done—and bad luck as always, the prodigal son was the "perfect" match. It was the only time in his life he could remember someone using the word *perfect* to describe something about him.

He was going to have to go find Pop, somehow reel him in to the hospital. Cricket had been right—he was going to have to think hard to keep up with the old man. Pop was sharp from years of business dealings—he was focused, determined and ornery. Fortunately, Jack knew something about determination.

He'd find him. Somehow, he'd drag him back.

CRICKET WENT to the Morgan ranch, pulling into the driveway in her old Volkswagen that had served her well for many years. The sight of the ranch and the large house that graced the property, out in the middle of nowhere, never failed to take her breath away. She parked, shut off her car, grabbed her tape measure and notepad. A promise was a promise. If Josiah Morgan was going to be on a first-name basis with the angels— unless he accepted his son's kidney, and if the operation and match was a success—she was determined he would come home to a pleasant-looking house.

No one answered her knock at the front door. Cricket decided she could call either Laura, Suzy or Priscilla and ask them to come let her in…or perhaps she could find an open door. If one of the Morgan men were here today working somewhere on the ranch, it was possible they'd left a door unlocked. They wouldn't mind her slipping in to measure, particularly as she'd mentioned her plans to Josiah.

She turned the knob.

Sure enough, it was unlocked. That meant one of the Morgans was nearby, so she carefully slid the door open and called, "Hello! It's Cricket Jasper!"

She waited for a "Hello, Deacon!" or something to that effect, but no one answered. Closing the door behind her, she walked into the hallway. "Hello! Gabe? Dane? Pete?"

All the brothers had moved into houses with their brides, leaving the ranch house to Josiah. Pete was the most recent to move, needing private space for his four new babies and wife. He and Priscilla had bought a house only a few miles down the road once the adoption was final, and Cricket was pretty certain Josiah had been crushed by the departure of the babies. "Anybody home?" she called.

Jack appeared in the hall like a ghost. "Hey, Cricket."

He startled her into the fastest heartbeat she'd ever experienced. "You scared me, Jack!"

He grinned at her. "I can't exactly claim that I'm home, to answer your question. But I'm here." He looked around, his gaze returning to the flat stare he almost always wore.

"So what are you doing here?" Cricket demanded, her heartbeat still jumping around.

"What are *you* doing here?"

"Measuring for drapes." Cricket slid past Jack, keeping an eye on him. After Josiah's warning about his son, Cricket had decided her unhealthy crush was something she needed to put away. The man was sexy, but as a deacon she had no business mooning after a hunk who had not one good side but two bad. "If you'll excuse me, I'll just measure, draw some sketches and go."

He caught her arm as she went by. Cricket jumped, snatched her arm back.

"Hey," he said, "I think you and I got off on the wrong foot."

"No," Cricket said. "We're fine. Let's not trouble ourselves about anything except getting your father well."

Jack looked at her, his gaze direct, sending a shiver over her. "I heard you telling a bunch of fibs to my father last night."

She shrugged, clearly not remorseful. "So? Is it wrong to want him to be happy? Is it sinful to put him in a happy frame of mind before he has major surgery?"

He eyed her. "A fibbing deacon."

She raised her chin. "Never you mind what's between me and the Lord, cowboy."

He grinned. "Your conscience is your own, my lady."

"Good." She started to turn away, but there was that hand again, holding her too close to him. She wished she didn't feel an unsettling sizzle everywhere he touched her. This time, she stood firm, refusing to allow him to unsettle her.

"And while we're examining your unusual conscience," Jack said. "You wouldn't help my father escape, would you, Deacon?"

Chapter Three

"What are you talking about?" Cricket demanded. "Escape what?"

"Pop left the hospital in the night. Checked himself out."

Cricket seemed to consider his words, doubting him. She finally said, "He was fine when I was visiting."

Jack shrugged. "Guess he changed his mind. Now I need to find him."

"Is he here?" Cricket's voice contained a dose of worry.

"No. Too obvious, though I was hoping he'd make it easy on me to take him back to the hospital."

Cricket held her notepad close to her chest. Perhaps she was afraid he might take a bite out of her, a very tempting thought—but he was no Big Bad Wolf, contrary to his father's opinion.

"If he doesn't want to go back, you can't make him."

Jack smiled. "Maybe you could give me your best thoughts on where he might be. My brothers haven't seen him, their wives haven't seen him. The logical conclusion was that he'd had a yen to see the grandchildren. Then we figured he might be here. No luck."

She shook her head. "I'm sorry I can't help."

Thunder clapped outside and a slice of lightning cracked near the house.

"My word," Cricket said, "that sounded close! If you'll excuse me, I'll take my measurements and let you get on with your search. I hope you find him, I really do."

Jack let her go. She didn't know where Pop was. Nobody had the faintest idea; no one even knew where all the properties he owned were. He could be anywhere in the United States. Pete had mentioned that he thought Pop had sold the knight's templary in France, but Jack supposed Pop could just as well have left the country. "He is the most difficult man on the planet," he muttered, along with a well-chosen expletive or three.

"Did you say something?" Cricket asked, madly scribbling numbers on her notepad.

"Nothing fit for the ears of present company."

She turned back to what she was doing. "I can't blame him, you know."

"Blame him about what?"

"He didn't want your kidney. He didn't want anything from you at all. I polished your résumé, tried to make it seem like you were the kind of son who—"

"I heard the polishing." Jack threw himself into his father's recliner. "Pop didn't believe any of that crap."

Cricket sniffed, went back to ignoring him.

"Where'd you stay last night?"

"With Pete and Priscilla and the four babies."

He watched her stretch to measure the length of the current rod, admiring her lean body as she moved. "Full house?"

"Yes," Cricket said. "I love being there. They can use the extra pair of hands, and I enjoy the fun." She stopped to look at him. "Have you even seen any of your nieces and nephews?"

"Deacon, look," Jack said, "I haven't seen my brothers or my father in years. Why on earth would I have seen their offspring, which, by the way, only became part of the family in the past few months?"

She stared at him. "Some people like to make up for lost time."

Her words needled him. She knew nothing about his family, knew nothing about him. He really didn't feel like he needed judgment from someone who was supposed to be fairly nonjudgmental.

"Nothing short of a wedding will bring your father back here," Cricket said, and Jack blinked.

"You don't have any children?" he asked.

"I most certainly do not." She bent down to examine the bottom of the windowsill and he didn't bother to avert his gaze from taking in a scrumptious eyeful of forbidden booty. "Anyway, what matters is whether *you* have any children. Your father lives for family."

"Jeez, don't rub it in." Darn Pop for being so difficult. He was almost tired of being lectured by Cricket, yet the instrument of his conscience-picking was at least attractive. Rain suddenly slashed the windows, and Jack noted the room had gotten darker. "When you plan for drapes, maybe something heavy enough to keep out the cold in winter and the heat in summer would be nice," he said, watching the rain run in rivulets down the wall of windows. "No sheer lacy things that just look pretty and serve little purpose."

"Oh?" Cricket straightened, much to his disappointment. "Planning on living here?"

"I don't think so," he said softly. "I haven't stayed in the same place for more than three nights in many, many years. That's not likely to ever change for me."

She looked at him, her gaze widening. It seemed to Jack that she reconsidered whatever she was about to say. Then she put away her things, allowing them to be swallowed by the enormous gypsy bag she carried, and said, "I'll be going now. It was good to see you again."

He laughed. "You are a gifted fibber."

"Just because I have good manners does not make me a liar."

"Whatever."

"I'll see myself to the front door."

He nodded amiably. "You do that."

She slipped past him, her carriage straight as a schoolteacher's. Because she was tall and lean, she moved gracefully, a sight he'd probably always enjoy watching. He really liked the way her dark hair fell around her shoulders, lustrous and probably softer than…hell, he didn't know what would be as soft as that woman's hair must be. It just looked silky, and it probably smelled good, too.

This train of thought was taking him nowhere fast.

He was behaving like an ass to Cricket, and Pop's disappearance wasn't her fault. Jack got up and followed her to the door, where she stood staring out at the rain-whipped blackness.

"You probably don't have a raincoat in that suitcase-sized purse of yours."

"I'll be fine," Cricket said. "You have enough to worry about without concerning yourself about me."

"I didn't say I was worried. But it didn't escape my notice that your tires are fairly bald, and your car is a tad past old, and the roads will be a mess getting up to the highway. In other words, drive safely."

She looked up at him. "My, aren't we the gentleman suddenly?"

He scratched his head. "Tell me again which church you serve as a deacon?"

"I never told you at all."

"That's true. I'm just curious what congregation would put up with such a—"

"Jack," Cricket said, "the only thing on your mind right now should be Josiah."

"I suspect he's not driving in this weather. Nor is he out in it," Jack said.

Cricket hesitated.

"This isn't going to be a popular theory," Jack said, "but I'm betting that little Beetle of yours with the gummy tires doesn't make it to the main road. You'll be calling someone to hitch you out of the mud in less than five minutes. I'm sure my father would suggest you stay put until the rain passes."

Cricket closed the door. "I'll accept your father's kind invitation."

He nodded. "I bet if we poke around in the kitchen we'll find something to eat."

"I'm not hungry, thank you."

That was too bad. He'd been hoping she'd be eager to show off some of her culinary skills. "You don't like me very much, do you?"

"Let's not make this personal," Cricket said, making herself at home at the kitchen table while Jack checked out the contents of the fridge.

"Not me," Jack said. "I'm Mr. Impersonal."

"Wonder where he is, anyway?"

"You'd know better than me." There was fresh turkey and cheese in the meat drawer, and Jack felt the evening was improving already.

"There's a guesthouse on the ranch, right? A few barns?"

"I've searched everywhere." Jack closed the door, leaving the food behind, suddenly lacking an appetite. He felt a confession coming on, and those were never very good for his gut.

Cricket watched him. "What are you doing?"

Jack took a deep breath, slid into the seat opposite Cricket's. "See, here's the deal. The old man was rough on us, me in particular. He wasn't the kind of father who'd play ball with you, he wasn't around much, he wore us out with his criticism. If I had a penny for every mean thing he said to me, I'd be a wealthy man, I promise. Me, more than any of my brothers, never measured up. And he hated what I loved most, which probably just made me love rodeo more. I didn't have to be good enough for Pop when I was riding—it was just me and the bull and hanging on for the sake of winning."

"So what happened?"

"He blamed me for a car accident my kid brothers had when they sneaked out to see me ride one night." He looked at Cricket, the old, painful memories rushing over him. "The thing that ticked me off the most was that I was crazy about my brothers. We felt like all we had was each other, and I basically got to be the father, in a way. I loved them. I would never have hurt them. I had no idea they were sneaking out to watch me that night." Still, the painful accusations cut. Remembering the beating his old man tried to give him hurt, too, but even more painful was the fact that he'd fought back. The two of them had gone at each other like prize-fighters, and Jack wasn't proud of it. "I suppose in the end I let him beat me," Jack said, "but I took skin from him before he did."

"I am so sorry," Cricket said, reaching across the table to pat his hands, which he noticed were splayed in front of him as if he needed the comfort. He moved his hands to his knees under the table, not wanting to appear as if he needed sympathy.

"I don't even know why I'm here," he murmured. But he did know, he knew he still loved his brothers, and Pop wanted those grandchildren, and if all it cost to make everybody happy—buy forgiveness—was a kidney, then that was cheap.

"Maybe you are a good man," Cricket said. "Maybe you really *want* to do the right thing."

He looked at her, then slowly shook his head. "I don't think so." He would never be good enough to live in her world. Repairing the cracks of his relationship with his family would take more than anything he had in his soul. Thunder and lightning cracked and boomed over the house, snapping the lights off. The refrigerator stopped humming. He thought he heard one of the many pecan trees that bordered the property give a tired groan, a warning that much more wind would drive it to split. "The lights'll come back on," Jack said to soothe Cricket.

"I'm not afraid of the dark."

Of course, she wouldn't be. She'd probably produce a glow-in-the-dark Bible from her purse, lead a few prayers, invoke the heavenly spirits for safety, and it would never cross her mind that the thing she should be afraid of was *him*.

Chapter Four

"I remember there was a flashlight somewhere in the kitchen." Cricket felt along the walls, wishing she could recall where she'd seen a plug-in flashlight. While she had to admit to a sneaky bit of excitement at being in total darkness with Jack, this was the type of thrill she didn't need in her life. "Aha!" Pulling it from the wall, she turned it on, flashing the light right at Jack's face. He was smiling, she saw, a sort of catlike grin.

"Feel better?" Jack asked.

"Since I don't see in the dark, yes, I do." How dare he pull on her heartstrings and then go alpha-jerk on her? He'd almost had her believing that he wasn't the prodigal his father claimed he was. She set the flashlight on the kitchen table. "Find another one and we'll each go our own way. I'll take Suzy's old room for the time being."

"Suzy's old room is where Pop was staying before he took off," Jack said.

Cricket replied, "Just tell me where you want me. I'll

be up bright and early, as soon as the rains quit, and gone before you know it." She wasn't certain she'd actually sleep under the same roof with Jack, in fact, wouldn't even consider it if the roads were better. "And this is a secret to be kept between you and me, if you don't mind."

He grinned. "Do I look like the kind of man who kisses and tells?"

She grabbed the flashlight. "If you have kissed me, it must not have been memorable. I'll take one of the rooms that hasn't been in use."

He followed her as she went up the stairs. "I'll sleep on the sofa downstairs. Feel free to yell out if you get scared. I'll be close by enough—"

She stopped and turned on the staircase, not a hairsbreadth away from him since he'd been following her, his eyes on her rump, if she had Jack Morgan figured correctly. "I can't see myself calling for you to rescue me from anything."

"Not even a mouse?" he asked, his eyes dancing with mischief.

"Mice?" she repeated faintly. "Do you have them?"

He shrugged. "I can't speak to the quality of the upkeep at the ranch. There were many months when no one was here, so I suppose there could be some furry residents."

"You're horrible," she told him. "You're trying to give me the shivers."

"You wouldn't be afraid of a tiny furry rodent, would you, Deacon?"

She snapped back around and marched up the last couple of stairs, heading into the first room she saw. It was empty except for a dresser and a bed, it had its own bathroom, and best of all, the door locked with a satisfying click when she shut it in Jack's face. "Jerk," she muttered. "What woman loves a mouse?"

"Good night," he called through the door.

"Good riddance," she replied, hugging the flashlight.

JACK WENT DOWNSTAIRS, moving around skillfully in the darkness, and clicked on the TV as he tossed himself into his father's recliner. Then he realized the TV didn't work at the moment. There was nothing for him to do, and that made him miss Cricket's lively banter, even if she was a bit vinegary for his taste. He liked his women a bit more sweet and willing, and if they threw in a little hero worship, that was even better. Yet Cricket didn't seem to feel any inclination to adore him, in spite of the fact he was willing to give his father a lifesaving kidney.

Cricket probably wouldn't be easy to seduce at all. He could spend months wooing her and she'd likely remain cold to his advances.

Why was he even thinking about sex with the deacon? He had as much chance of that as…well, as finding Pop tonight.

He was forced to admit that he was worried about his father. The crusty old man was going to die for his independence. Secretly, Jack admired that. He understood the desire to go down fighting.

Suddenly there was a flashlight beam at his elbow and a tap on his shoulder. "Holy smokes!" he exclaimed, jumping to his feet. "Cricket! I didn't hear you leave your room!" How she'd made it down the stairs without even a creak, he couldn't imagine, but maybe thin frames like hers didn't put pressure on the floorboards like four rowdy boys could.

"I didn't mean to startle you," she said.

He took a deep breath to calm his racing heartbeat and sat down in the chair again. "Is there something you need? If there are no towels in the bath, you can probably—"

"I want to apologize for my behavior," Cricket said. "I've not been very nice to you, and you have a lot on your mind. I should be more considerate of your feelings."

Great. Now he was a pansy. "I'm fine."

"I think…I think I'd feel better if I sat down here with you for a while."

"I was just kidding about the mouse," Jack said, feeling bad for taunting her.

"I know. But if you wouldn't mind company—"

"Oh, sure, sure." Jack waved at the sofa. "Help yourself. Nothing good on TV, anyway." He winced at his weak joke.

She hesitated, and then to his great surprise—astonishment—Cricket reached out a hand toward him, the hand not holding the flashlight. Was she going to conk him with it? Jack stared up at her, perplexed by her actions.

She didn't say anything, just looked at him.

Then he got it.

Cricket wanted him. Or at least she didn't seem to want to sleep alone.

He took half a second to consider whether he should do this to the deacon—perhaps she was afraid of the dark, lonely, having a bad-girl fantasy, whatever—then threw any guilt out of his mind. Pulling her down into his lap, Jack kissed her the way he rode bulls, full out and with every intention of staying in the saddle for as long as he possibly could.

WHEN CRICKET AWAKENED the next morning, she blushed at the memory of the wild night she'd shared with Jack. If anyone had ever told her that lovemaking was such a fabulous, heart-pounding, please-don't-stop experience, maybe she wouldn't have waited so long. But she had, she'd always been waiting for Mr. Right. Last night, although she knew Jack was no Mr. Right, she'd decided she was tired of waiting for the prince who might never ride into her life.

It had been worth it. It could even be addictive, which was not a healthy thought. She slipped away from the sleeping cowboy on the floor in front of the fireplace. The fire had burned low now, mostly just embers, but outside, the sky was dawning clear and crisp. The roads, though still muddy, would be passable.

She tried to figure out how to escape without waking Jack. The last thing he would want was a girl-friend, and most people who made love together might assume there could be some kind of ongoing relation-ship. She didn't relish him thinking that's what she wanted from him. At least she'd accomplished her goal, which was to understand what other women who fell in love were so happy about. It was hard to understand the giddy excitement over men and sensual pleasures when she'd never experienced it. Now she had, and she totally understood why women could fall so hard for the wrong man, and also why they could love one man all their lives. If she could enjoy the giggling, the excitement, the tears of joy and rapture, the feeling of living outside of her body that she'd experienced with Jack, she'd love the man she married with devotion all her life, too.

So if she never saw Jack Morgan again, she'd be okay with that. A practical girl understood the cards she was dealt. She'd counseled plenty of women who'd had their hearts broken by Mr. Wrong, all the while hoping he was Mr. Right. Cricket would never fall victim to a lack of common sense.

Today it was back to her church for her, and no more mooning over the dashing cowboy who'd no doubt broken a hundred hearts. She gathered her clothes and crept into the hall to quickly dress, glancing back over her shoulder at Jack partially wrapped in the blanket. She prayed the front door would open and close without him hearing—it did—and ran to her VW. The car vroomed to life, and she headed toward Fort Wylie with only a slight regret that she wouldn't see Jack again, at least not the way she'd seen him last night.

Last night's indiscretion was the only time she was

going to allow herself to live outside the bounds of good moral direction, she promised herself firmly.

JACK HAD SLEPT with enough women to know that it was a good thing if they didn't stick around for the difficult details of goodbye. Still, he was disappointed, and even ego-bruised, when he found Cricket had departed. Had she regretted last night? Wasn't he the lover she'd wanted? Doubts assailed him, a rare occurrence. He didn't like wondering about his performance. It was much more fun when women made him feel as if he was the greatest stud on earth.

In fact, Jack almost felt as if he'd been dumped. Dumped by the deacon, and refused by his father.

His father was understandable. They'd never been close, even though it was a reasonable assumption that a man who had so much to live for would be grateful for a kidney. After all, Josiah had given him life; Jack felt that returning the favor was good for his heavenly record. But no, neither Josiah nor Cricket seemed to feel the need to give Jack a little reciprocal gratitude.

He didn't feel it would have been too much to ask of Cricket to hang around, make him some eggs, act appreciative, maybe even slightly worshipful. She was very difficult to understand, and he didn't like that. Women shouldn't make a man think too long and too hard; otherwise it took all the fun out of the pursuit.

Her hair had been every bit as soft as he'd imagined, and her skin had smelled sweet, like roses and strawberries. It had been a gentle, clean fragrance that made him burrow his face against her neck, her breasts. Her touch had driven him completely insane.

He had never, ever, had a woman leave him without saying goodbye. He had always been the one who'd left. There was something final about a woman who departed of her own accord; it left the other player no moves on the chessboard.

At least the electricity had come back on this morning. Jack grabbed the blanket off the floor, where they'd made love in front of the cheery—and romantic, if he did say so himself—fire he'd built in the fireplace. A strange spot on the blanket caught his eye; dumbly he stared at the stain. And that's when he realized that Cricket Jasper had been keeping secrets. She hadn't offered him the slightest clue that she'd been a virgin, which felt somehow as if she'd cheated.

She wasn't a virgin anymore. Now it stung like crazy that she hadn't hung around for a goodbye kiss. Jack felt worse than at any time in his life, even when he'd been thrown flat on his backside—and maybe even stomped— by an assorted collection of ill-tempered bulls, as he tossed the blanket into the washing machine.

Cricket's desertion served as a reminder of the other people in his life who seemed to move on without saying goodbye. He didn't have to put up with this crap. After he'd tidied up the place so that no one would ever know he'd been there, Jack grabbed his stuff and headed back to the one place he knew was a safe harbor—the rodeo circuit.

Chapter Five

"Marry me," Josiah Morgan said to Sara Corkindale, the kind social worker who'd helped his son Pete and his daughter-in-law Priscilla adopt quadruplets last month. "Marry me and put me out of my misery."

Sara laughed. "I'm not willing to be a secret bride, Josiah. And if you *are* at death's door—as you've claimed you are, I suspect, to get sympathy from your family—why should I make myself a widow again? I've already done that once, and it's very hard to say goodbye to a good friend and husband. Why would I marry you knowing you're ready to hang up your spurs?"

He shook his head. "I like you," he said simply.

"And I like you."

She patted his arm affectionately in a way that was not at all condescending. Josiah hated everybody tiptoeing around him and treating him like an invalid. Sara made him feel as if he still had something to offer a woman.

"You'd like being my wife even better." She didn't seem inclined to bend to his way of thinking, so Josiah considered his other options. As he had moved himself into her house, where he knew none of his sons or their wives would think to look for him, he didn't have many options. He was rather at his hostess's mercy.

"You're going to have to tell your children where you are eventually." Sara looked at him with a gentle smile as she put a fresh-baked pound cake on the table, and then picked up her knitting. "If I marry you, they'll say I took advantage of you."

"No one has ever taken advantage of Josiah Morgan!" This was a fact; his sons wouldn't dare suggest it because it would be ludicrous. "I'll marry when and who I want."

"You can't hide behind my skirts, Josiah," Sara said, and his jaw went slack.

"Sara Corkindale, I should take you over my knee and spank you for suggesting I'm a coward." He thought about doing it and decided he didn't dare. Hide behind her skirts, indeed! No one had ever suggested he might be a bit thin-skinned and he rather admired her spunk.

She held up her work. "This is a baby blanket. It's going to be blue and white, and warm enough for winter's chill."

"It better not be for me," he said darkly. "Sara, I'm a man, not beholden to anyone."

"This blanket is for one of the babies at the orphanage. There are never enough warm things. And I know you're a man, Josiah, but you know you're hiding here when you should just express your opinion to your sons. If you don't want to have the kidney operation, then say so." She went on with her knitting serenely. "In the meantime, you can't stay here forever."

"I can't?" Josiah had gotten used to the comfort and peace of Sara's home in the past few days. He'd gotten used to the calm way she went about her business. In his mind, he'd envisioned himself living here until the end of his days.

She shook her head. "No, you can't. Not until you straighten your life out with your children."

She was still worried someone would think he'd been coerced into marrying her. She didn't understand that no one had ever made him do a thing he didn't want to. When Gisella had left him, there hadn't been a durn thing he could do about that, but still, that had been Gisella's choice. He'd always respected her decision, knowing he'd been at fault. But that hadn't been coercion; he'd become a single father because he'd been a bit of a ham-handed dunce. "Are you saying that once I tell everyone I don't want the surgery, that what I want is to get married, you'll marry me?"

She stopped knitting and looked at him. "Josiah, I would marry you if you were going to be around a while."

"Nothing's certain in life."

"I know that. But you seem determined to have an expiration date stamped on you, and it's hard for me to want to get married knowing that." She swallowed, chose her words carefully. "Don't ask me to care about you and then say goodbye to you in less than a year."

She had a point. Suddenly, he didn't want that, either. It would be horrible, holding her at night, watching the stars with her, seeing the sun come up in the morning with Sara, and knowing each sunrise might be his last.

"I still don't want to do it," he said quietly. "My son is reckless. He'll always be a hell-raiser. Sara, you don't know my boy, but Jack…Jack deserves the chance at the kind of full life I've had. And nothing's ever going to stop him from rodeoing, not even being minus a kidney."

"You'll have to stop trying to live everyone's lives for them, Josiah," she said, pulling her chair close to him. She put her head on his shoulder. "Our children have to make their own choices."

"So you're saying I should accept one of his body parts and then just sit around and wait for the phone call that he…he's gone to the great rodeo in the sky?" He didn't think he could do that. Some things were too awful to contemplate.

"Or you could accept his gift, and then go watch him ride as often as you can," she said.

"Watch him ride!" Josiah exclaimed. "Not durn likely!"

"Have you ever seen him ride?"

"No, and I ain't gonna start now!" Josiah felt an urge to yell, but knew he better keep his voice down. This was a lady's home, and he respected Sara too much to yell. But for pity's sake, the woman asked a lot of a man.

"I'll go with you," she said softly, and he melted like a pile of snow in August. "And I'll take you back to the hospital, too, so that they can finish looking you over. I think you'd want to do that. I'm sure you've scared your kids half to death."

"All right," he said, surrendering. "That's the first time in my life I've ever been sweet-talked into anything, you know."

She kissed his cheek. "Didn't it feel good?"

He felt like warm dough under her benevolent, cheerful gaze. "Yes," he said, "it felt mighty good."

IN THE LAST TWO MONTHS Jack had been to South Dakota, North Dakota and a few other states, chasing buckles and trying to forget Cricket. He hadn't heard from her, not that he'd expected to. It was crazy how he couldn't get the deacon off his mind.

He hadn't heard from stubborn old Pop, either. He had a new cell-phone number, so his brothers hadn't been able to reach him. Now that it was May and he'd ridden off a lot of angst, he'd had time to think about everything.

He wondered if Pop was still as opinionated as the devil. His brothers would have gotten word to him through the circuit if Pop had passed. Still, a strange itch tickled at him, telling him it was time to call home.

He called Pete. "It's Jack," he said.

"Jack," Pete said, "are you all right?"

"I'm fine. Just checking in."

His brother hesitated. "Where are you?"

Jack squinted at a sign he was parked under. "Somewhere in the Dakotas."

"Coming home anytime soon?"

"Not sure." Jack scratched his head. "Should I?"

"I don't know," Pete said, "but I think Pop wants to get married."

"He does?" Jack blinked. "How?"

"By a minister of some sort, I imagine."

"But last time I saw him, he was in a hospital."

"Yeah, and he maybe should still be in one. But Sara Corkindale, his lady friend, keeps him perked up."

"That's good news." Jack really didn't know what more to say. "When's the wedding?"

"I believe after he has the kidney operation."

Jack's eyes went wide. "You mean he's changed his mind?"

"She's changed his mind, more to the point. But I think the window of opportunity is closing."

Jack got the point. "I can be home in two days. Maybe less."

"I'll tell Pop."

"Hey," Jack said before Pete could get off the phone, "you haven't happened to talk to that preacher woman lately? Has she been by to visit the quads?"

Pete cleared his throat. "You haven't. Why should she?"

Damn. He hadn't seen them since he'd visited Pete at the hospital. Never held them, never touched them. "Man, I'm sorry. I'm an ass of an uncle."

"I won't tell them that," Pete said, "but I bet they'd

like having an uncle around who can teach them how to ride a horse."

"That's a few years away, isn't it?" Jack frowned. Would they even be walking by now? He had no frame of reference for how fast children developed. They'd been in bassinets at the hospital when he'd seen them three months ago—had it been that long already?

"Time flies," Pete said.

Jack replied, "Okay, what are you hinting around about?"

"Not me," Pete said. "I'm not hinting about a thing. Would never spill any beans. Know how to keep my mouth shut. You just get home, and everything will take care of itself."

Jack grunted as the phone line clicked dead. What the heck had that been all about? Starting his truck, he turned due south and headed home to Texas.

CRICKET COULDN'T BELIEVE how ill she felt. Pregnancy was supposed to make a woman glow; all she wanted to do was gag. She couldn't seem to catch her strength. Priscilla Perkins had sold her house to Cricket when Priscilla married Pete Morgan and Cricket felt at home in her new sanctuary, but she hadn't felt well enough to enjoy it in the past month. She'd hoped one day to reopen the cute little tea shop that was part of the house, but now she realized her hands were full for the moment. Her life was changing fast, and nothing was ever going to be the same.

She was scared. Questions tormented her. She loved

the idea of being a mom, but at the same time she dreaded having to tell Jack. Before too much time passed, sharing their news was a fact she was going to have to face. There was no reason to feel too guilty right now about avoiding her confession; she'd talked recently to Suzy and Priscilla on the phone and each of them had mentioned that Josiah never had his operation, and Jack had taken off for parts unknown. No one knew where he was—he'd never even visited any of their homes or seen their children before he left.

They'd pretty much given up on him. As for Josiah, he'd made it plain he was going to live his life his way.

Cricket had another confession to consider—she'd also have to tell her church. While she didn't dread that as much as telling Jack—Jack was in for a life change he didn't want—the congregation was sure to be shocked. She hoped they wouldn't think worse of her, but her behavior would certainly strike everyone as embarrassing. They would want her to resign, of course. Her parents might be ashamed, and her brother was sure to be disappointed.

The bright spot in her life was that, like Laura, Suzy and Priscilla, she would have her own child. She'd told her friends, swearing them to secrecy, and they'd assured her they wouldn't breathe a word to Jack. Motherhood was the most wonderful thing to imagine, if she wasn't so worried about telling Jack. There was no way of knowing how he'd react, but she had a feeling it wouldn't be the best news he'd ever gotten.

It was time for her prenatal checkup, so Cricket

locked up her lovely new house and left. Cricket wanted to ask the doctor if there was anything she could do about the nausea—eat better, drink something more healthy, anything to make her more comfortable. Fortunately, there was a wonderful selection of teas still in the cupboards of the shop. She was eating holistically, when she had an appetite—organic fruits, some yogurt, whole grains and chicken that was free of hormones and preservatives. Nothing helped.

An hour later, Cricket knew the nausea wouldn't be passing any time soon.

"Triplets!" Dr. Suzanne exclaimed with delight.

"Triplets?" Cricket's heart sank, her skin turning cold and clammy. "Do you mean three babies?"

"That's what I mean." The doctor smiled. "You've always been an efficient person, Cricket. You'll have a whole family all at once."

Cricket endured the gentle teasing silently. She couldn't talk. "Are you certain?" Nothing on the monitor looked like triplets to her.

"Three tiny heartbeats," the technician confirmed.

"It'll be quite a lot to ask of your thin frame," Dr. Suzanne said. "Bed rest will be required at some point, so you need to prepare for that. Get what you want done accomplished soon. And be thinking about some type of help while you're housebound."

Cricket closed her eyes, blinked, stared again at the monitor. She couldn't tell anything by looking at the screen, but the technician and doctor seemed quite convinced they were looking at triplets.

It was the craziest thing she'd ever heard. There was no way, it just couldn't possibly be true. She wanted to laugh, she wanted to cry, she had to lie on the table for a few long moments, shocked beyond anything she could have imagined.

If Jack had been the slow one among his brothers to start a family, he was about to make up for lost time in rapid fashion.

"I don't know how to tell the father," she said to the doctor, and her doctor smiled sympathetically.

"He'll be thrilled, Cricket, after the shock wears off."

Cricket wasn't sure this kind of shock was something that would wear off. Jack had never wanted to be a father. "Can you tell if they're boys or girls?" Cricket asked. She didn't know which Jack would think was worse.

"He'll love babies of either sex," Dr. Suzanne assured her. "We might be able to tell at a later sonogram, but it's still a little soon. For now, though, everything looks just right."

Cricket dressed and left, not completely comforted. Jack Morgan lived for rodeo; he wouldn't be planning diapers into his cowboy lifestyle.

And then a big smile lit her face. "I'm having triplets," she murmured. Never mind what everyone else might think about her condition. It was the most wonderful thing that had ever happened to her. "Thank you, Lord," she murmured, trying to decide who to give the good news to first.

Chapter Six

"This is not good news," Jack said, staring at his father. "You haven't been doing anything the doctor asked of you."

"I took a small sabbatical from good advice from doctors," Josiah said. "It's good to see you, though."

Josiah knew he was supposed to stop drinking whiskey. Sara had made him quit. But four days before the newly scheduled surgery, Josiah had started again. Jack suspected his father was nervous though he'd never admit it. "How the hell do you expect to get through this in the best possible shape while you're doing that?" Jack demanded.

Josiah raised a brow. "Since when did you become the parent, and I the child?"

"Since you started behaving irrationally. Let's have the bottle, Pop."

Josiah handed it over. "It wasn't any good, anyway. I've lost my taste for it, which is aggravating. And I think it's all Sara's fault."

Jack looked at his father. He half believed him. Josiah didn't exactly look like a shiny new penny, rather one that had seen its fair share of pockets and hard wear. "What's the matter, Pop?"

"Ah, hell if I know." Josiah scratched his head. "Don't like feeling like a baby."

"Babies have a good life." Jack tossed the bottle in the trash. "Enjoy the attention for a while."

"All right." Josiah sighed. "I'll give up the bottle, and you give up the rodeo, and we'll both suffer loudly together."

Jack considered his father's words as he stared out the hospital window. Life was tricky and weird. He really didn't feel like riding anymore, though he wasn't about to say so. Like Pop with his booze, rodeo just didn't have the same taste to him anymore. "We'll get through this, Pop," he said.

"See, that's the thing," Josiah said. "What if we don't? What if I let you do this, and something goes wrong?"

"Like what?" Jack glanced at his father.

"Like maybe the damn surgeon doesn't know what he's doing and he doesn't do you a good surgery. Maybe your body doesn't like having one functioning kidney and decides to go off. What if the one kidney you have left isn't a good one, and they gave me your best one?"

Jack shrugged. "Let's not borrow a lot of trouble, Pop."

"We need that praying friend of yours," Josiah said. "Deacon Cricket. She could sit at our bedside and bend the good Lord's ear on our behalf."

Jack sighed. "We can take care of ourselves."

"Speak for yourself. I like the way she coddles me. Give her a call."

He'd like to, but he wouldn't. She'd call him if she wanted to talk to him. After all, she'd left without so much as a "thanks, muffin." He'd replayed their time together over and over, and he couldn't think of a way he'd gone wrong. He'd finally consigned Cricket's silence to regret. She simply wished she hadn't made love with him, probably felt she'd done something wrong.

As many times as he'd replayed that night, all it got him was restlessness and cold showers. His skin was going to permanently prune if he didn't stop thinking about her. "I'm not calling her," he said.

"I'll do it," Josiah offered, "if you're too chicken."

"Pop," he said. "I'm so chicken I could be plucked of feathers. But don't call her."

"I won't," Josiah said, "but I will confess to making a different phone call that I think will surprise you."

Jack looked at his father, waiting.

"I called your mother the other day," Josiah told him.

Jack didn't want to go there. "That was a long time ago, Pop. No need to open that wound."

"She's still your mother."

Jack sighed.

Josiah didn't say anything else, which was a sign he wasn't pleased with Jack's reaction. "I guess the obvious question is, why did you feel the need to call her?"

"Sara suggested I should," Josiah said.

Jack looked out the window again, wishing the

surgery was over already. He didn't want to be here. He wanted his father well because it was the right thing to think. And then he wanted to be gone again. Anywhere, nowhere, just not here.

"Sara said it was time to put the past to rest. Gisella probably misses you boys. And Sara and I talked about how bitterness breaks families in strange ways. Since we're having life-altering surgeries, it's best not to go into them with negative memories." Josiah smiled when Jack turned back to study him. "Sara works for child welfare services, you know. She knows a lot about what makes families tick."

"I'm glad you're happy, Pop." As far as Jack was concerned, his mother had chosen to leave and never come back. Never sent gifts, never wrote. He wasn't going to worry about what made families tick when the maternal clock had been broken for years.

"There's such a thing as forgiveness being good for the soul," Josiah said.

Jack frowned. "If I'm going to forgive someone, I'd start with you."

Pop's eyes bugged. "You wouldn't give me a kidney and hold a grudge, would you?"

Jack shrugged. "Holding grudges is part of our family identity. I learned it from you."

"I don't know if I want you giving me a kidney that's full of grudge," Josiah said.

"Quit trying to weasel," Jack told his father. "We're going to have the surgery this time, we're going to do it together, and we're both going to be happy about it."

"Not so much," Josiah said. "You boys ride me terribly, but I wasn't that lousy of a father."

"Don't sell yourself short." Jack sighed. "Hell, it doesn't matter anymore. Let's just live for the future."

"Glad you suggest it. Your mother said she'll be here soon enough."

"Why? There's nothing she can do."

"She wants to see all the grandchildren. She wants to see her boys. Said she wanted to meet the wonderful woman who talked me into getting off my high horse and calling her." Josiah's eyes grew misty. "Funny thing about your mother, she has a heart of gold. I wish I'd appreciated that when I was younger. It's something you miss out on about your wife when you're busy trying to make a living."

Jack blinked. "Are you going to marry Sara?"

"Yep," Josiah said, "just as soon as I'm well."

"Our family tree is odd," Jack said. "There's a lot of twists among the branches."

Josiah shrugged. "Every family has its twists and unique branches, son. The fact that we keep fertilizing the roots is what makes our tree strong."

"Oh, hell," Jack said. "Next you're going to be after me to do some fertilizing. Pop, kids is one thing you're never going to get out of me, so don't even start the chorus."

"Excuse me," the doctor said as he came into the room, "I'm Dr. Goodlaw."

Jack stood, shook the doctor's hand. "Jack Morgan."

"Ah, Mr. Morgan's eldest son."

Jack nodded.

"Well, I have an unusual bit of news," Dr. Goodlaw

said. "We just had a kidney come up that is a match for you, Mr. Morgan."

"What does that mean, exactly?" Josiah's brows furrowed.

"It means that this particular kidney is from a young accident victim whose parents want his organs donated. He was healthy and active, and his family would like to know that his organs are helping other people to live healthy, active lives. I know you have a family match who has offered, but I recall you didn't elect for surgery under those conditions."

"No, I did not," Josiah said with a stern glance at Jack. "I don't elect, not one bit."

"It's up to you, Mr. Morgan, although a decision will need to be reached fairly quickly. There are other recipients in the registry, of course."

Jack and his father looked at each other. Then Josiah shrugged. "I don't need any time to think it over. I'll take the kidney."

Dr. Goodlaw nodded. "I'll go make the arrangements." He shook Jack's hand, then Josiah's. "This will move fairly quickly."

"Good," Josiah shot back. "I'm tired of feeling like I'm at everyone's mercy."

The doctor smiled and left the room. Josiah refused to meet Jack's gaze. Jack knew exactly what his father was thinking: *I owe nobody nothing.* Jack couldn't say whether he felt any particular relief that he wouldn't be giving up a part of his body. "Are you all right, Pop?"

"I'm fine," Josiah said. "As fine as anyone can be who just had a miracle thrust upon them."

"What do you mean?" Jack went and sat by his father.

"I prayed I wouldn't have to take your kidney. I couldn't stand the thought of you rodeoing with one kidney. I just don't want to outlive my kids," Josiah said. "Now that I've got my boys all around, I'd like to get to know you."

Jack felt honest emotion jump inside him. He looked away, cleared his throat. "I almost like you better when you're being a jackass."

"That's because I'm an enemy you can keep fighting against. You like holding grudges. But you won't get any fight out of me, son. I'm getting a young person's kidney, and I'm going to take full advantage of the spark it gives me. You're off the hook."

Jack shook his head. "You just didn't want anything from me."

"True." Josiah closed his eyes. "I don't want you doing anything for me that you don't really want to do."

"I didn't mind, Pop."

"I know you didn't mind the surgery, and I thank you for being willing to make the sacrifice. But I think it's better this way."

"Okay, Pop."

Josiah took a deep breath. "And since I'm wiping slates clean here, I guess you'll be wanting your million dollars."

"Not if it comes with a wife."

"It doesn't. But you do have to reside at the ranch, same as the other boys did."

"They didn't stay a year!"

"No, but they did get married, have families. They fulfilled what I wanted, which was to get along with each other, bring some harmony into our family."

"Pop, I was going to give you my kidney. I've visited you often in the hospital. That's pretty harmonious for us."

"Yes," Josiah said, "but it's your brothers I want you visiting."

"I will, Pop, I will."

"It won't hurt you to hold some babies, get to know your nieces and nephews," Pop nagged.

Jack held up his hands. "Pop, you're about to have surgery. We can talk about this later."

"We can talk about it now. Is it a deal or not?" Pop demanded, and Jack looked at his father.

"Why are you so hopped up about this all of a sudden?"

"Because I'm about to have complicated surgery! It's not like getting a hangnail removed. I need to make a phone call to my lawyer. I have to make sure all the family matters are tended to just in case my old body doesn't like young, healthy kidneys!"

Jack held up his hands. "Hang on, Pop, relax. Don't give yourself high blood pressure or they won't operate. What exactly is it that you want from me? Where do I sign on the dotted line so that you can cool down?"

"You have to stay at the ranch for a year, get to know your brothers, be a family. Same deal they got."

"And if, just if, a wife and family comes into the picture? Does that abbreviate the deal?"

Josiah sniffed. "I make those decisions when they occur. Depends on many factors. Do I like your choice of bride? Am I really getting grandkids? Are you improving your life? Being a good uncle? I don't want you loafing around the ranch for a year, biding your time just to get my million bucks. I don't want you forwarding your mail to the ranch and saying you live there. In other words, I wait and see what I'm buying before I pay."

"I don't really need a million dollars, Pop," Jack said. "I'm pretty happy being free."

"Yeah," Josiah said, "you're my hardheaded son."

Jack grinned. "I'll do this on one condition."

"I'm living with Sara," Josiah said. "I'm not insisting upon this because I need you to be my nursemaid."

Jack shook his head. Pop was the most stubborn human he'd ever met. "You don't start sending a bunch of women to the ranch to try to settle me, thinking I'll give up rodeo just because you find me a wife."

Josiah shook his head. "I would never do such a thing."

"You're fairly relentless in your pursuit of the perfect family tree."

"Not me," Josiah said. "I don't believe there are perfect family trees. But I do think wives are a durn good thing. Bring a man a lot of good stuff he never knew he was missing."

Jack shook his head. He tried to decide if he could

stomach a year of family, and then he thought about Cricket.

Maybe it wouldn't be so bad to live in Union Junction for a year. "Where do I sign with my blood?"

Josiah rubbed his hands. "It's a gentleman's verbal agreement. Now get out so I can call my lawyer. I have to hurry because Dr. Moneybags may be here soon to take his pound of flesh from me."

"I guess I'll go check out the cafeteria."

"Good," Josiah said, reaching for the phone. "Find a cute nurse while you're in there. There's lots of them around here."

Jack headed to the cafeteria with no intention of taking that advice. He had one woman on his mind—and that was plenty.

He dialed up his brothers and let them know Pop's news. Then he drummed his fingers on the table, watching people move around with trays. He couldn't say he wasn't relieved not to be tied by an organ to his father. It felt as if they were coming to some kind of agreement between them, something almost resembling respect.

Since he was going to be a resident of Union Junction for a while, maybe it wouldn't hurt to call a certain deacon and let her know that he'd be living close by, just in case she was interested.

But what would he say? *I heard you bought Priscilla's house and tea shop in Fort Wylie, but I wish you lived in Union Junction so I could see you occasionally.*

There was no point.

Chapter Seven

There were many details Josiah needed to wrap up before he went under the knife. Nothing was going smoothly with Jack, as it had with his other sons. They'd fallen in with his plans after a hiccup or two, but Jack was no closer to finding his way home to family than before. He was really worried about how Jack would accept Gisella. Josiah understood that his eldest son had always been a sincere loner, and if anything, anything at all got ticklish between he and his mother, Jack would disappear. No million dollars would bring him back. Jack lived in a world of his own creation.

Josiah knew why this was. As soon as Josiah got out of the military, he'd begun his lifelong goal of acquiring business and property. He was determined to deserve Gisella, give her everything she didn't have.

But Josiah was moody, struggling with start-up businesses. He and his wife fought a lot. Gisella hated being left alone on the ranch; she was afraid of the dark. Their few cattle started disappearing and Gisella was always edgy, afraid the boys would have a run-in with some dangerous rustlers. Gisella was from France, and English was not her first language. She had no female friends where they lived out in the country to make her feel less isolated.

He was gone on a business trip to Dallas when he got the worried call from Jack. All of eight years old, Jack tried manfully to tell him his mother was gone— in the end, he dissolved into tears that Josiah would never forget hearing him cry.

His eldest son would never forgive his mother for deserting him. Jack had barely forgiven Josiah for the rough treatment Josiah had felt Jack needed to handle the hard knocks life was sure to mete out. Josiah wasn't sure he'd made the right decision with Jack. His eldest was almost too tough now, emotionally locked up. Nothing really penetrated his stoic approach to life.

Jack was likely to find a reason to skip Gisella's visit altogether. Josiah had pondered this, giving it great thought, and hatched a plan. There weren't many second chances in life, but he really wanted mother and son to have one with each other. He suspected that if this bond wasn't recreated, Jack would never be able to maintain a loving, giving relationship with a woman. Josiah hated that he cost Jack something in life that gave a man great pleasure.

Josiah hoped Gisella and Jack would both forgive him for what he was about to do—but it had to be done, for the sake of the family.

TWO HOURS LATER, Gisella walked into the room unannounced. Grouped around Josiah's bedside were Gabe, Dane, Pete, their wives and Jack. Sara Corkindale was there as well, giving Josiah the comfort he had learned to expect from her calm presence. No one recognized Gisella except Josiah, and he felt the familiar flash of joy at her beauty and bearing. Time had not changed her cruelly by etching wrinkles on her face. He saw that she was smiling at him as one did at a long-lost friend. He hoped they could be friends after she learned what he had done.

He was about to be prepped for surgery and there was little time for fretting about the past. "My sons," he said, "this is your mother."

It was as if a stone dropped from the ceiling and landed in the room. No one went to hug her. The brothers stared at her so finally Gisella moved forward, giving Josiah a gentle kiss on the forehead. "You look well, Josiah, for what you have been through."

"I hope I look as well tomorrow," Josiah said.

Gisella looked at Sara. "You must be the wonderful woman who convinced Josiah to call me."

Sara smiled, and the women shook hands. "I'm sure you know that no one can convince Josiah of anything unless he is already convinced of it himself."

Gisella laughed, a full-throated sound Jack remembered from his childhood. It came upon him with a wild, stinging sensation that he'd never gotten over missing that laugh. He had never gotten over missing her. As a boy, he couldn't understand why she'd left him, what he'd done wrong.

Gabe went and hugged Gisella. Dane followed and then Pete. Jack scowled, wanting to hang back, but after the wives had been introduced, Jack realized the time had come. "Mother," he said, barely kissing her cheek.

She smelled fresh, like spring roses, and it occurred to him he'd missed that smell. Painful memories rushed over him.

"I can see my little man has grown into a big man," Gisella said. "I've thought about you often, Jack."

"Yes, yes," Josiah said, interrupting the homecoming, to Jack's infinite relief. "And now that your mother's here, there's some tidying up to do. Best to get these things done in case I croak under Dr. Moneybag's good care."

"Pop, there's no point in getting worked up about things that can wait. We're all shell-shocked to see Mom. Let us enjoy her for a moment," Pete pointed out, but Josiah waved an impatient hand at him.

"A man doesn't go to his grave with a messy conscience," he said, "not unless he's an idiot or run out of time, neither of which applies to me. Sara, may I have the box, please."

Sara produced a shoe box from her handbag and handed it to Josiah.

Josiah sniffed, then looked at Gisella. "Gisella, on many counts I was not a good husband."

"On many counts, you were," Gisella returned. "I

was not the perfect wife. There is no such thing as perfection in a marriage."

"I like her," Sara said. "She understands family."

"I pick good women," Josiah said gruffly. "Sara, you might as well know this about me along with everybody else. Boys, in this box are all the letters your mother sent you over the years." Josiah pulled the top off the box. "You can see that none of them have been opened. I could have read them to you since I speak and read French, but I chose not to out of a stubborn sense of pride and misplaced pain. For this egregious misdeed, I apologize to you all and humbly ask for forgiveness."

Gisella's eyes sparkled with tears. For the first time, a little forgiveness toward his mother seeped into Jack's heart. "Pop," he said, "that's kind of brutal, don't you think?"

Dr. Moneybags came into the room to make certain his patient was being prepped and to give his soothing pre-surgery talk. "Doc," Josiah said, "I need ten more minutes before you roll me to the gallows."

"Mr. Morgan," Dr. Goodlaw replied, not sure whether to be offended or not, "I assure you we have an excellent team to perform this surgery. It is not a gallows situation."

"Ten minutes is all I need, please, Doctor. And I meant no offence to your skills."

The doctor nodded. "The next time I see you, you'll be asleep. Do you have any questions?"

Josiah looked around the room at his sons, their wives and the two women in his life. "Do I need much more reason to wake up after surgery with a grin on my face?"

The doctor smiled and left. Josiah let out a sigh. "Gisella, I owe you an apology. Many actually. I was mad when you left. It doesn't excuse what I did. It doesn't save me from the damage I inflicted upon our children. I hope you can forgive me."

Gisella started to say something, but Josiah waved her quiet. "Hang on a minute, there's more," he said. "The Christmas and birthday presents she sent you for many years were given to charity. I'm sorry. It was a selfish thing to do, more than selfish."

Jack stared at his father, looked at his mother, who seemed fairly upset but not necessarily destroyed by his father's confession. Then Gisella went over and kissed him again on the forehead.

"You are too hard on yourself, Josiah," she said. "You are a good man. Let's not think about the past anymore."

"Well." Josiah sniffed. "I was still an ass."

"I knew that about you when I married you. I didn't want a man who wasn't strong." Gisella smiled. "It takes a very strong man to ask forgiveness."

"Yeah. I guess. I have a lot to ask." Josiah looked around the room. "So, I have one more thing to tell the assembled family. By the way, I would like to see everybody together again and not necessarily on my deathbed next time—"

A general groan broke out in the room.

Josiah nodded. "Jack's going to reside at the ranch for a year."

"I'll *try* to," Jack interrupted.

"In order to earn his million dollars, he'll do it," Josiah said, ignoring his son's words. "However, I have begun the paperwork to cede the ranch to Gisella. It is now hers to do with as she sees fit, although it cannot be sold until after Jack completes his quest. Gisella, one year from today, you may sell it if you wish. I'm sorry I didn't give you the home and the love you needed when we were married, but now I hope to make up for that." Josiah looked at all his children, his gaze stern. "And I expect everyone to remember that my driving force is family. Visit your mother often."

He sat up and looked at Sara. "Get the nurses. I'm ready to be split open like a turkey at Thanksgiving."

She smiled at him. "Your family members may do it for you," she said sweetly.

"And that reminds me, no lawsuits over the land or ranch," he said, wagging a finger at all of them. "Or you forfeit your portion of my will, little as it may be after Dr. Moneybags takes his chunk. Is that understood?"

Everyone murmured a shocked assent except Jack, because he didn't need anything, money or land, from his father. Thankfully, he was tied to no one.

"Jack?" his father said. "This means more to me than a kidney."

Jack looked at his father a long time. Then he glanced at his mother, whose gentle smile beamed on him so warmly that it was difficult to continue being a hard case. "Sure, Pop, whatever."

Laura, Suzy and Priscilla went to hug Gisella and

welcome her to the family. After a moment, the brothers did, too. Except Jack, who decided not to get caught up in the sentimental moment. It wasn't the time for him to live in the Hallmark-card family moment, no matter how much Pop wanted it.

Nurses entered the room to wheel Pop out. Jack's throat closed up. The feel of family, of being hemmed in, of life being out of his control, threatened to overwhelm him. He needed some separation.

He needed to ride. It was the only thing that would make him sane right now, feel in control. "Be well, Pop," he said, gritting his teeth as his father was wheeled down the hall to presurgery. They all watched as a suddenly silent Josiah was taken away. Gisella and Sara wiped away surreptitious tears, sitting down together side by side. Jack cleared his throat, realizing he, too, was tearing up with nervous emotion. This was awkward. He looked at the box of old, unopened letters on the table, a silent testament to Josiah's stubbornness. A ranch had been given to his mother with the proviso that Jack could live there with her for a year. What the hell was that if it wasn't a trap laid by Pop? But Pop didn't understand that the past couldn't be laid to rest with a quick apology and a confession.

"I'll be back," Jack stated, and left the room.

Maybe he would, maybe he wouldn't.

Chapter Eight

Jack didn't get far. He bumped into Cricket, who was hurrying into Josiah's hospital room.

"Oh, my," Cricket said, glancing around. "I missed him, didn't I?"

Laura, Suzy and Priscilla came over to hug her.

"Josiah just left," Priscilla said. "But you'll be here when he wakes up, and that will make him happy."

Jack stared at Cricket. She looked different. For one thing, she was wearing a dress that brushed her calves, and boots. Since it was chilly today, he understood the need for warmth. But she also looked different somehow, in a way he couldn't explain. Glowing. Was she glowing? Perhaps it was the nippy air that had put the sparkle in her eyes.

"This is Gisella, mother of the Morgan brothers," Priscilla said, and Jack realized he'd forgotten his manners. He just couldn't seem to catch up to the speed of events in the room.

He joined the group. "Gisella, this is Cricket Jasper from Fort Wylie."

"Hello," Cricket said. "It's so nice to meet you. I've heard a lot of wonderful things about you."

Gisella smiled at her. "Thank you."

Cricket glanced around, her gaze settling on Jack. "I'm sorry I wasn't here in time to pray for Josiah."

Jack shrugged. "No problem."

"Your father called me yesterday," Cricket said, "but I'm a slow starter these days. I meant to be here earlier."

Suzy smiled at her, then patted Cricket's stomach. "You look beautiful."

Jack hesitated. No woman patted another woman's stomach, then told her she was beautiful unless she wanted her hand chewed off. Women and weight was a personal thing…unless…Jack stared at Cricket, shock spreading over him. Belatedly, he realized Laura, Suzy and Priscilla were smiling at him, watching his reaction. Cricket simply looked worried.

She *couldn't* be pregnant. Jack shook his head to clear his brain. His brothers shifted uncomfortably and Jack felt faint, as if he'd been thrown off a bull and hadn't landed quite right. "Cricket, you're not…is there something I should know?"

Cricket hesitated. "I was going to tell you, but—"

"Oh, jeez." Now that he looked at Cricket's waist and stomach more closely, he could see the obvious.

"We're having a baby," Cricket said, her face red. "I meant to tell you sooner, but—"

"Pete, scoot that chair behind Jack before he falls," Gabe said. "I remember when I found out I was having a baby. I felt like my boots weren't attached to the floor for a minute."

"I hope that meant you were happy," Laura said.

Gabe eyed Laura's enormous pregnant stomach. "Every day," he said. "It feels like I'm waiting for Christmas."

Jack sat in the chair Pete moved behind him. Then he jumped out of it, too stunned to sit. He couldn't take his eyes off Cricket. Was she really having a baby? *His* baby?

"This is so exciting," Gisella said, clapping her hands. "I'm going to be a grandmother again, and this time, I'll be here for the big event. Two," she said, with a proud smile at Laura, who looked as though she might give birth any day.

This could not be happening. Jack inhaled deep breaths to brace himself. "I'm going to be a father?"

Everyone laughed. Cricket smiled at him for the first time since she'd entered the room.

"Yes," she said softly, "to triplets, actually."

Jack couldn't move, he couldn't speak. Never had his life rushed so fast, not even the eight seconds he rode to the buzzer. This was different.

This was a crazy ride.

His brothers congratulated him, pounded him on the back, shook his hand. One of his brothers mentioned something about "nice shooting, bro," and general guffaws broke out. Gisella kissed Cricket on the cheek, and Sara smiled.

"Josiah's going to have such a gift when he comes

out of surgery," Sara said. "He'll be so excited he'll probably recover twice as fast."

Jack tried to say that he was excited, too, but all that came out of his mouth was a rusty croak no one heard over all the sudden hugging and kissing of Cricket. Jack knew he needed to say something to her, act pleased, brag like an expectant father—but all he could do was try to keep his knees from knocking together and suck air into his lungs.

He'd never been so scared.

How could he—a man who spends all his time on the rodeo circuit—be a father? To triplets?

He had no home. He basically lived out of his truck. The rodeo circuit was his family. He had no steady employment, no way of caring for a wife and three children.

The obvious smote him—he was going to have to live on the damn ranch, prey to his father's manipulations, in order to earn the million dollars Josiah had set out as bribe money. It was fast dough, and he'd need it pronto if he meant to be something other than a loser father and shiftless husband. He stared at Cricket, realizing his whole life was changing, and he'd have to change with it.

"I'm thrilled," he said. "This is great."

CRICKET KNEW JACK was anything but "thrilled." He looked pale, maybe even sick. It was a lot for him to take in on the day his father was having surgery. She wondered if he'd known Gisella was coming home and decided he had enough to bear without finding out he was a father. She forgave him for his lack of real enthusiasm, remembering that she'd had a few moments of shocked doubt before genuine happiness washed over her.

Still, she wished she and Jack knew each other well enough to be truly excited about being parents together. She wouldn't have come today had Josiah not called her, asking her to be there before he was taken into surgery. As it was, she'd missed him leaving and felt bad about that.

She'd known her secret might be out when Jack saw her, and tried to camouflage her pregnancy with a dress. He might not have figured it out had her good friends Laura, Suzy and Priscilla not given him a broad hint even Jack couldn't miss. She would have preferred to tell him herself, when they weren't surrounded by people, and when Jack wasn't worried about his father.

But now he knew.

"A wedding," Gisella said with delight. "Josiah didn't tell me the good news. When's the date?"

Cricket glanced at Jack, stricken. She didn't know what to say. She understood why Gisella might have misunderstood that there was to be a wedding, but—

"As soon as Pop's well," Jack said, shocking Cricket. "I imagine he'll be on his feet fairly quickly, don't you? He's a fighter."

"Indeed," Cricket said as Jack walked over and planted a kiss on her lips. "Can I talk to you a moment— outside?" she asked as everyone in the room was celebrating the idea of another Morgan wedding.

"Sure," Jack said, putting his arm around her. "Keep playing along with me. You're doing great."

She didn't like the sound of that. She'd heard that sneaky tone used before, but always from Josiah. "What are you up to?" she demanded when they were safely in the hospital hallway.

"You've got to save me," Jack said. "Pop's trying to trap me."

"Look here," Cricket said, already feeling heat run under her good sense. "I refuse to be regarded as a trap, Jack Morgan. You are not a rabbit that I set out to snare, for your information."

"Oh, hell, no, I didn't mean that." He held her against him, kissing her as Pete glanced out in the hall.

"Just checking to make certain you lovebirds hadn't flown the coop," Pete teased. "Mom's planning a huge wedding, just so you know. At the Château Morgan, which is to say the ranch. She has visions of you in a formal suit," he whispered to Jack so their mother wouldn't hear. "All the weddings she missed is making her want a doozy."

"Thanks for the warning," Jack said, waving his brother away. "Look, you can see what's happening here, can't you?"

"Not exactly," Cricket said. "I have a lot on my mind these days and haven't been focusing on the Morgan family, at least not the ones in Union Junction."

"Precisely my point," Jack said. "Pop's moved Mom onto the ranch. He's turning over ownership to her. I'm supposed to live there for a year with her to get my million dollars."

"What million dollars?" Cricket asked.

"All my brothers got a million for coming home to Pop. It was bribe money," Jack explained. "Now he's brought Mom into the picture because of his guilty conscience. None of my brothers had to live with her, though, and put up with Pop, and learn how to be a father all at once. The deck is stacked against me. I'm going to need your help, Deacon."

"I'm not a deacon anymore," Cricket said, detaching herself from Jack's arms. She was reluctant to part from him but she didn't want to be part of a cover-up. "I wasn't really deacon material considering my unwed, pregnant state."

"Oh," Jack said, "a little too rebellious for the church, huh?"

"I consider myself to be, at the moment, and turned in my resignation to spare them having to ask me to leave." Cricket was terribly embarrassed by this. "Anyway, I'm not the person you need to talk to about any type of help. My days are spent warding off morning sickness."

"Marry me," Jack said. "We'll ward off a lot of things together."

She looked at him, wishing the proposal was offered seriously. He was so big and tall, handsome in a devil-may-care way. She knew this man was too much of a rogue to ever be tamed by a deacon and three babies—she wouldn't dream of getting involved in his scheme. "I can't, Jack. Don't ask it of me."

"Sure you can," he said. "Save me, I'll save you."

"But I don't want to live at the ranch. I mean, I like Gisella, she seems like a woman who's eager for a second chance. You need to spend some time developing that relationship," Cricket said, sort of realizing the wonderful madness behind Josiah's scheme. "You should obey your father, you know."

"You mean for the money."

"No," Cricket said. "Although that's definitely a plus. But your father knows what he's doing, he almost always has."

"Oh, you weren't here for the fireworks," Jack told her. "There's a box sitting in there full of letters Mom sent us over the years that Pop never opened. He's a stubborn old fart, and he let her suffer, and us. The only reason he's springing all this now is he's genuinely afraid of pushing up daisies after this surgery. I don't think I ever saw Pop take anything stronger than an aspirin."

"He had his own medicine," Cricket reminded him, and Jack nodded.

"True, but you get my point. Pop was scared silly of giving over the control of his body and his life to a surgeon. He felt like he had a lot of cleansing of his conscience to do. I'm okay with that," Jack said, "but I don't want him running my life so that his conscience is clear."

"What exactly are you proposing?" She looked up at him, wondering if Jack realized just how much like his father he was turning out to be.

"I don't exactly know," Jack said. "I'm working the details out on the fly, but it goes something like this. I have no prospects—some money put away, no job. No debt. No house. Am not especially close to my family. Not quite sure what I'm doing in life other than pleasing myself."

"So, as potential marriage material, you're not exactly a shiny catch."

He grinned. "That's a fair statement."

"Okay," Cricket said. "Again, you have to live at the ranch to earn your keep. I don't want to live there."

"We can live in the guesthouse," Jack offered. "It's big enough to raise a family in, and be private, while sticking to Pop's rules."

"This is going to sound crazy," Cricket said, "but I'm not marrying you for money."

"I wasn't exactly suggesting you should," Jack said, but Cricket shook her head.

"That's what it comes down to. You need money, so you want to marry me. The only reason you're propos-ing to me, Jack Morgan, is that I've got the three magic tokens that will push you into doing what your father wants. Otherwise, you'd just as soon walk away from any amount of money."

"This is true," Jack said. "Being a father does change my perspective. I don't want them growing up without a parent like I did."

"Oh, gosh," Cricket said, "you are a tangled web of insecurities and emotional angst."

"Yep," Jack said with a grin. "Part of my appeal."

"I wouldn't exactly agree, but I shouldn't have let you sweet-talk me into bed," Cricket said, knowing she was fibbing like mad. She didn't regret a moment of their time together.

"Ahem," Jack said, politely catching her in her re-telling of who had instigated their lovemaking.

"Here's the deal—I just bought Priscilla's house and tea shop. I was always enchanted by her house and the business. I admired her ability to make a business out of almost nothing. So when she wanted to sell it to come live in Union Junction with Pete, I jumped at the chance to buy it from her. I suppose maybe I knew somewhere in my heart that I wouldn't be a deacon forever." She looked up at him, hoping he'd understand. "My life's changing pretty fast, Jack. A tea shop is something I can do as a single mom and still be at home with my children. Do you see why I don't want to leave Fort Wylie?"

Jack stared down at her, nodding. "Yes, I do," he said. "It's crazy, but it just might work."

"What?" Cricket demanded. "What just might work?"

"I'll be a tea-shop cowboy," he said with a wink and a grin, "Coffee, tea or me?"

That would cause a stir. There'd be more women hanging around the tea shop and her cowboy than she could bear. Cricket raised a cool brow in response to his deliberate teasing. "I don't think you could handle the heat in this kitchen, Jack Morgan."

Chapter Nine

Jack knew the moment Cricket said she didn't want to leave Fort Wylie that he had to convince her to let him live in her world. It was the only practical solution that solved everything except money.

"A million dollars is a lot to give up, anyway," Cricket told him, all teasing spirit fleeing. "You'll resent me later for missing the opportunity of a lot of wealth."

Jack shrugged. "Don't try to understand me and we'll both be fine."

"It's not a matter of understanding you," she shot back. "It's a simple matter of understanding human nature. I don't see you being happy passing out cookies and cakes to moms with school-age children."

"It was your idea," he said, and Cricket blinked.

"How so?"

"You're the one who said it was the perfect way to be a stay-at-home parent, and that's what I'd like to do." Jack kissed her on the nose. "Two can live as cheaply as one. Surely five will be a snap."

"You haven't done much grocery shopping lately." Cricket shook her head. "Jack, do not use me and the babies as an excuse to get out from under your father's thumb."

"A thumb is a terrible thing to be under," he said.

"You're just exchanging his thumb for mine. Eventually, that's the conclusion you'll come to."

"You make me sound shiftless," Jack said. "I'll have you know, I'm responsible to a fault."

"This is a bad idea," Cricket said. "Even in my less-wild dreams, I thought my marriage would be more about love and less about business."

"You wanted to be an excellent businesswoman," Jack reminded her. "I'm just offering a partnership since we've already started parenthood together."

He had a point. The blue-ribbon prize she barely allowed herself to contemplate was that she'd win the rodeo man she wanted if she went along with Jack's proposal—and wasn't that worth doing for her children?

She looked at Jack's long, lean body and wondered if she was really thinking about her children or herself.

"So you'll marry me, Cricket?" Jack asked.

"Perhaps," she said, still worrying about the wisdom of marrying a man who'd never wanted to be married. "Something tells me nothing good can come of this. No tea-shop cowboy for me."

Jack grinned. "You make getting married sound so dangerous."

She looked at him—and wondered.

IN HIS SLEEP Josiah was visited by ghosts. Or maybe they were angels, he couldn't be certain. They floated into his subconscious, three strong, lean, well-muscled Templar knights dressed in armor, looking very much like pictures he'd seen. Only these knights were serious, annoyed and bored, clearly out of sorts to be on this particular quest. He hoped they were angels coming to rescue him from his plight, but the possibility that he deserved disheveled, disheartened ghosts more than angels couldn't be overlooked.

"You abandoned us," the one he named Serious complained. The man could use a good shave and a respectable haircut. "You left us in the templary without so much as a kind word."

"Sorry," Josiah said. "I wasn't aware you were there."

"You wouldn't have said goodbye anyway," Bored said. "You don't like to say goodbye."

"It's a bad habit," Josiah agreed. "Why are you here?"

Annoyed looked at him. "For moral support. You asked for guidance and comfort, so here we are."

"I don't remember that," Josiah said. Maybe he had. He'd been terribly nervous about the surgery, a fact he hadn't wanted to share with his family since he felt he always had to keep the tough-old-lion face on.

"We wish you hadn't sold the templary," Serious said. "You didn't even give us a quest."

"Aren't you on one now?"

Bored waved a chalice at him. "This is a snap of the fingers. We need something important to do."

"But I'm pretty sure you're a figment of my drug-induced fears. Dr. Moneybags loaded me up pretty good on antianxiety dope, though I told the nurse I wasn't anxious. I'm more pissed than anything." Josiah felt that was a waste of his hospital bill. An aspirin was likely to cost fifteen bucks, never mind the amount of tranquilizers it would take to "antianxiety" him.

"We think we'll move onto the ranch with you," Annoyed said.

Josiah said, "I won't be there. Only my eldest son and his mother will live there."

Bored scrabbled around in his tunic for something, booze Josiah figured, to fill his chalice. "I'd help you out with that but they took my whiskey from me," Josiah said.

"Listen," Bored said, "a knight has to fight. It's what we do. You never gave us anything to fight for. We need you to figure that out now."

Josiah blinked, shaking his shaggy head. "I don't have anything to fight for."

"Aha!" Serious exclaimed. "But you do. You wanted this family. Now you have to stick around to raise it."

"I'm trying to," Josiah said. "Can't you see I'm getting a new kidney?"

Bored scrunched his face. "Good to hear that you have no plans to chicken out just because your son is."

"What does that mean?" Josiah demanded.

"It means Jack plans to be married at cock-crow in a faraway town," Annoyed said, "to a woman of prayer."

"Cricket," Josiah said. "That's a good thing."

"Nay," the annoyed Templar said. "He plans to move away, thereby thwarting your wishes."

"Has he no respect for his mother?" Josiah demanded, and Bored hunched his shoulders, probably depressed about his empty chalice.

"He is farther away from her than ever, and therefore you—" Bored said "—you forced him to go away."

"Look," Josiah said, "I'm just trying to keep my family together."

Serious nodded. "Follow us," he commanded.

"Where?" Josiah asked, feeling a twinge of fear. Should he be journeying with ghostly knights while he was being operated on? It didn't seem to bode well. They appeared as real as Dr. Moneybags and just as unpleasant, as far as Josiah was concerned. Why would he conjure up imaginary companions at this late stage of his life, when he had everything he wanted?

"Follow us," Serious repeated, and Josiah left his body and followed his trio of knights.

"This is the Cave of Fears," Serious told him as they stood inside a strange cavern of many colors. "You have to face fears or they become your reality."

"Shoot," Josiah said, "I'm not worried about my fears. They work themselves out in time."

"Because you avoid them," Bored said. "You can't avoid the fear of your son leaving you for good."

"Oh, hell," Josiah said, "I'm too tired to face that fear. Can't I beg off?"

"Knights don't beg," Annoyed intoned, "and you

were born to be a knight. You raised your sons to be stronger men than you had been."

"I was born to be a knight?" Josiah asked, suddenly feeling stronger.

"What did your father and mother tell you?" Annoyed asked, his face etched by a scowl.

"That big boys don't cry," Josiah said, remembering. "But I cried often."

"Why?" Annoyed asked him.

"Because I hated being alone. I wanted brothers and sisters." It was painful remembering living alone in the country with no siblings. He'd never gotten over the loneliness, never.

"Face your fears in order to finally live the life you want. You have to change, not change your sons," Serious told him, and the three knights disappeared.

"Mr. Morgan," a faraway voice said. "Mr. Morgan?"

He blinked his eyes. His eyelids were almost too heavy to open. "I'll just nap awhile longer," he told the insistent voice, "if you'll be kind enough not to pester me."

"Mr. Morgan, you came through the surgery just fine," the voice told him, but Josiah knew he was really on the brink of his last chance at being the father he'd always dreamed of.

JACK WASN'T SURE how his mother could forgive his father for secreting her letters over the years—he wasn't sure he forgave Josiah for that. It would have made a huge difference in how Jack had perceived himself. He'd always thought it was his fault his mother had left, though later on in life he'd known that was not the case. Still, as a child, he'd only known she'd left, and he hadn't been able to keep her from going. He watched his siblings file in one at a time to visit Josiah and wished he was off in a bedroom with Cricket somewhere. The strangest itch had come over him to feel her stomach. He wanted to touch the soft mound where his children were. When would they kick? Were their hearts beating yet? He had no idea about babies. He supposed they did whatever they liked, whenever they liked. Cricket sat beside him anxiously watching the doorway, completely unaware of his proudly possessive paternal thoughts that soon turned to a more lustful nature.

He was in trouble. Maybe she didn't want to make love with him anymore. He had gotten her into quite the jam. Though his brothers congratulated him for his "good shooting," the fact was, she wouldn't be sitting there contemplating the hugeness of triplets if he'd obeyed the simple rule: *No love without a glove.* Among his friends on the rodeo circuit, everyone promised themselves they could touch, but not without proper protection.

He wondered if she would have ever come to him on her own to tell him about the pregnancy. Cricket was pretty independent. She had her life all set up without him.

Now that he knew, he had no intention of missing a moment, not one expanding pound, of her pregnancy. Naked, as much as possible. "Cricket," he said suddenly, "let's go."

She turned, staring at him with astonished eyes. "We haven't seen your father yet."

"He's going to be fine," Jack said, but Cricket shook her head.

"Relax, Jack, this family stuff isn't going to kill you." She patted his arm and turned back to staring at the hallway, waiting for one of his brothers to come out and share some news about Josiah. Laura, Suzy and Priscilla sat nearby her, clearly already counting her into their circle. He was the only one who was antsy.

It was probably because his mother sat with the women. Her boys were waiting their select turns to see Pop. Sara sat near Gisella, but Jack hung back.

"Hey," Pete said suddenly, sticking his head through the doorway, "Pop wants to see you, Jack."

Jack blinked, startled. Cricket squeezed his arm to comfort him. "Sure thing, Pete," he said, not wanting to seem like a wuss, and walked into Pop's recovery room.

He wasn't really prepared for the sight of Pop so still, so groggy. His father barely opened his eyes, but when he saw Jack, he made more effort.

"Jack," he murmured.

"Take it easy, Pop," Jack said, trying to ignore all the emotions suddenly swimming around inside him. "You need to rest."

"Don't leave," Josiah said.

Jack hesitated. "I'm right here."

Josiah barely shook his head. "Don't leave Union Junction. Don't leave the ranch. We need you here."

Oh, boy. Pop had no idea what he was asking. Maybe it was the drugs, or the new kidney talking. "Hey, Pop," he said, "you go back to sleep, okay?" He backed away from the bedside, wondering how his father had known he planned to forfeit his million dollars. He had to marry Cricket; he needed to be in Fort Wylie with her. Pop would just have to understand.

Josiah watched Jack's retreat through half-lidded eyes. "Please," Josiah said, and Jack didn't think he'd ever heard his father use that word to him in all his life.

Chapter Ten

Cricket saw the change in Jack the moment he left his father's hospital room. Jack made a beeline for her, grabbed her by the hand, barely said goodbye to his siblings and mother and Sara and left as if his heels were on fire.

"What's going on?" Cricket asked. "We need to stay here with Josiah."

"We need to go home and let you rest," Jack said.

"What happened in there? Is your father all right?"

"He's all right," Jack said. "He's not going to be any different because there's a young kidney inside him."

"Then why are we leaving? It feels like we're ditching the family when they need us the most."

"No." Jack looked both ways before he dragged her across the street. "Visiting hours are over, I promise."

"Then I need to head back to Fort Wylie. I have a lot to do."

"Great. Where are you parked?"

"Right here." Cricket stopped, looked up at him. "Are you all right?"

"I've never been better." Jack gestured at the car. "I think it's best if I drive you home."

"No," Cricket said. "I'm fully capable of driving myself. And you can drive your truck home to your ranch and do what your father asked of you."

"I'm going with you," Jack said.

"No," Cricket said, her tone as stubborn as his, "you're not dealing with your mother being here."

Jack shook his head. "What does that mean?"

"It means that you only want to marry me to get out of what you need to do. It's the big excuse, Jack."

"I'm going to be a father. I don't think there's anything disingenuous about marrying the mother of my children."

"Maybe not with anybody else, but with you, it is." Cricket looked at him. "Prove that you're not just running off with me like I'm your new rodeo gig."

"That's not fair," Jack protested. "And besides, how would I prove that I'm not avoiding something?"

"Tell me what your father said to you in his hospital room," Cricket said.

Jack's eyes hooded. "He said he felt fine."

"And?" Cricket was positive she was onto something because he was acting like a snake, coiled and waiting for danger to pass him by.

"I don't remember."

"I believe that," Cricket said. "And I believe that there'll be a lot of things you conveniently forget when we're married."

"You don't have a very high opinion of me," Jack said.

"On the contrary. I admire a man who constantly backs down."

His gaze narrowed. "No, you don't."

She raised her brows. "Tell me what happened in there, and don't tell me nothing did, because it was obvious by the way you flew out of there that something had."

Jack sighed. "This isn't going to work if you keep trying to read my mind."

She tapped a toe, waiting.

"Pop said," Jack told her reluctantly, "that he wanted me to hang around. He said he needed me here."

Cricket gasped. "And you're trying to hoodwink me into giving you a ride out of town! Shame on you, Jack Morgan! Your father said he needed you!"

"Yeah, but that's Pop," Jack tried to explain. "In the last year, he decided he needed all of us. He doesn't really *need* us. He's just—"

"A man who wants his family around," Cricket said. "Jack Morgan, how could you desert your father?" She stared at him. "It doesn't bode well for our future, that's plain to see."

"It has nothing to do with our future," Jack said, grabbing her and kissing her until Cricket thought her breath was going to give out. It was a wonderful kiss, a soul-stealing kiss, and Cricket very much wanted to fall in with his plans and let him hitch a ride in her Bug to Fort Wylie.

But she knew this was a pattern with Jack.

"That's what bodes well for our future," Jack told

her. "I'm going to kiss you every day of your life, there's not going to be a day of our married life when I don't."

Cricket shook her head. "I'm not marrying you. You can't desert him in his darkest hour."

"Pop always has dark hours when he's trying to get what he wants!"

"We just can't do this while he's recuperating." Cricket got into her car, rolled down the driver's-side window. "You stay here and take care of family business. I'll be back in a few days to hang drapes."

He noted her change of subject and sighed. "Pop gave the ranch and land to Gisella. You probably better check with her about curtains and stuff."

Cricket nodded. "I will. It'll give us a chance to get to know each other, which will be a pleasure."

"I want you to get to know *me*," Jack said.

Cricket started the engine. "Marry in haste, regret at leisure," she told him. "Bye, Jack."

Jack stared after Cricket as she drove off in the little Volkswagen. She thought he wanted to be with her to get away from Pop. And his mother. His family, in general.

She was right.

He got in his truck and followed her.

CRICKET WAS COMPLETELY aware that Jack was following her down the highway. In a way, she hadn't expected anything less from him. Jack lived by his own rules. This time, however, he was going to have to bend, although she had to admit to a tingle of excitement that the man was so persistent in his pursuit of her. She had never been the object of a man's focus before, and the fact that the man was Jack would be enough to make her pulse pound with giddy pleasure under normal dating circumstances.

Yet they weren't dating. They were rushing down the road toward parenthood, which for Cricket took some of the romance and giddiness out of the equation.

By the time she got to her house in Fort Wylie, she'd figured out what she was going to say to him. *Go home, Jack, we need some time apart.*

"Hey," he said, pulling up next to her and getting out of his truck, "if you invite me in, I'll buy you the biggest diamond I can find in Fort Wylie."

Cricket shook her head. "I don't need a big diamond."

"For triplets, you do. I'd say you deserve a medal of honor."

She put her hands on her hips. "Jack Morgan, sweet-talking me isn't going to get you in my house. I need to be alone for a while."

"Why? I can be good company, sometimes."

"While that may be true, I suffer terribly from morning sickness. You do not want to be around for that."

"I'll watch TV. Don't worry about it." Jack grinned. "You think I've never seen a sickly woman before?"

"I'm not sickly!" Cricket frowned at him. "I'm pregnant. This phase will pass eventually, according to the doctor."

"Let me carry you over the threshold," Jack offered. "I need practice for carrying you over when we get married."

Cricket opened her front door and waved him in. "I don't want to be carried."

"You're not the most romantic girl," Jack told her as he scooped her up anyway and set her gently down in the foyer. "I'm a romantic guy, however."

"It can't all be your way," Cricket told him.

Jack sighed. "True, otherwise you'd be a lot easier to get along with. I never thought that the woman I asked to marry me would turn me down. It's a blow to my ego, I don't mind saying."

Cricket turned on a few lamps, filling the room with soft light. "Make yourself at home on the sofa in front of the TV, keeping your hands to yourself and your thoughts fairly pure."

"Wow," Jack said, "did that come out of the *How To Scare a Guy To Death* dating guide or something that deacons keep on hand for couple's counseling?"

Cricket sighed. "I'm going to change into something more comfortable."

"That sounds more promising." Jack sat on the sofa.

"If you think baggy kimono robes are promising, you may be in for a surprise. It's hardly Victoria's Secret."

"Next time," Jack said. "Anyway, I could romance you if you were wearing a paper bag. As a matter of fact, I'd find that really sexy."

Cricket shook her head and slipped into her bedroom to change. All the talk of marriage was making her nervous. "Was your father in a lot of pain?" she called to him from the bedroom.

"No, he's just a pain," Jack said. "It'll take more than surgery to slow him down."

Cricket wrapped the silky kimono robe around her, found some cozy slippers—not the high-heeled mules a woman who had a hot cowboy in her living room might prefer—and put her hair up in a ponytail. She walked back into the living room, finding Jack lounging on the sofa, staring at the ceiling. "Cowboy, what are you doing?"

"Thinking about how strange life is. Did you ever think when we met that we'd end up together?"

"Absolutely not. You weren't in my car twenty seconds and I knew you were bad news." She went into the kitchen, fishing around for some tea and crackers. "You should have stayed with your father," she said as Jack followed her into the kitchen.

"I should be with you," Jack said. "You're having my children. My father is merely having fun planning my future."

"Was he?"

"He never takes a break from plotting." Jack ran a hand through his hair and seated himself on a kitchen bar stool. "I need to meet your parents, you know. I'm very behind in my duties as a father."

"Oh," Cricket said, "I guess."

"Hey," he said, "I'm going to get my feelings hurt if I continue perceiving a decided lack of enthusiasm on your part toward my courtship."

"I'm sorry." She set a glass of tea on the counter that separated them. "I've got motherhood on the mind, not matrimony."

Jack drank some of the tea. "If you were counseling us as a deacon, what would your advice be?"

She looked at him. *I'd want to say, "Girlfriend, you better hang on to that sexy cowboy with all your might."* "I'd advise that rushing into things is a bad idea when two people don't know each other very well."

He shook his head. "Terrible advice."

"What would you say?"

He hopped over the counter, landing in front of her, and took her in his arms. "I'd say get me in bed as often as you possibly can, you lucky woman. Life's too short to miss out on the good stuff, and I am definitely good stuff."

Chapter Eleven

Cricket awakened the next morning with a deliciously warm, strong cowboy wrapped around her. Jack's arm was tucked around her waist, keeping her tightly against him. She could feel muscles, hairy legs, a strong chest up against her, and then something moving in the bed, jutting up against her backside insistently.

"Good morning," Jack said, and Cricket hopped out of bed with a gasp, running for the bathroom.

"Was it something I said?" he called after her.

Cricket slammed the bathroom door, locking it before getting into the familiar position she assumed every morning. She would have been humiliated, but she was too sick to care.

Ten minutes later, she dragged herself out of the shower and slipped back between the sheets. Jack placed a ginger ale beside her bed, along with a rose. "Where did you get all that?" she asked, reaching gratefully for the ginger ale.

"I moseyed over to the store while you were showering," he said tactfully. "I remember Mom giving us ginger ale when we had upset stomachs."

She studied him as he lounged on her bed with a newspaper, completely unconcerned about her performance in the bathroom. She'd probably been making horrible noises in there, and he didn't seem to care. Some of the awkwardness she felt about being pregnant slipped away from her. "I'd offer you breakfast—"

"Don't even think about it." Jack waved a hand at her. "I grabbed a doughnut while I was out."

"Ew," Cricket said. "If I was in a different place in my life, I'd make you an omelette."

"If you were at a different place in your life, I hope you'd offer me seconds of what I had last night." Jack grinned at her. "You're a lusty woman, Deacon, a very positive side of you that I never would have anticipated."

She blushed. "Lusty may be too strong a word."

"Enthusiastic, then." Jack put away the newspaper.

"I have to go," Cricket said.

"Where?"

"I have things to do."

He stared at her, waiting for more information. She sighed. "I have a doctor's appointment this morning. Then I plan on driving back out to visit your father."

"You can't keep doing that," Jack said. "You need to rest my children."

"They like the busy schedule. And soon enough I won't have that much time to visit Josiah, anyway. The doctor says I'll be confined to lying around in the not-too-distant future."

Jack thought about that. "Cricket," he said, "we need to pick a home. This dual-town thing is going to get old quickly. We need to be settled for the sake of the children."

She waved her hand at him. "I mustn't be late. Let me show you the door."

"Okay," he said. But he waited until she was ready to leave herself, then followed her to her car.

"No," she said, "you are not coming with me."

"I need to start learning about this pregnancy stuff. It'll be good for me to ask the doctor some questions."

Cricket shook her head. "Jack, I don't need any help just yet, thank you. Your father is the one who needs your help."

It was obvious he didn't like that answer, but neither could he argue with the truth. "At least let me wait outside, and then drive you to Union Junction," Jack said.

"No," she said firmly. "Jack, go your own way like you always have."

It felt mean to leave him standing there, because he was so convinced he was trying to do the right thing by her. She didn't want the "right" thing—she wanted something else from him, though she hadn't quite figured out what that was. The man had a lot on his plate right now, and she was pretty certain he was using her pregnancy as an excuse to get out of facing family matters at home.

"Cricket!" he called after her. "You're the most sexy, beautiful woman I've ever had the pleasure of arguing with!"

Cricket watched Jack through her rearview mirror. The man had made love to her last night so gently, so sweetly, that she knew she'd never be able to keep him out of her bed if he wanted in it, which was quite the dilemma for a woman who knew she had no business loving a man who possessed a wild heart.

TWENTY SECONDS LATER, Jack turned, shocked that Cricket was pulling alongside him as he walked to his truck. He looked at her in her little Bug, wondering if she'd ever let him buy her a truck. There was no way she was going to be able to haul all the children he intended to have in that tiny, bubble-shaped vehicle. She didn't know it, but she was a big truck girl.

"Hey," she said.

"Hey, you," he replied.

"If you really want to come to the doctor with me, I guess that will be all right."

He grinned. "Couldn't live without me for a second, huh?" Jogging around the vehicle, he hopped in. "I knew you'd find me irresistible."

She drove off. "Fathers should participate."

"Glad you came to that conclusion." He really was.

"And on that topic," she continued, and he waited for the real reason she'd come back to pick him up, "it sort of comes to me that I might not like rodeo any better than your father does."

"That's not true," Jack said. "I met you at a rodeo. You must have some fondness for it."

"I met you when I picked you up hitchhiking,"

Cricket reminded him, "something I hope you're giving up."

"You're so cute when you're possessive," he teased.

"Let's not digress," she said, and he sighed.

"I don't see myself giving up riding," he admitted. Yet he sensed this was a test, a crossroads that Cricket might hold against him. He'd have to tread very lightly.

"This is why I always recommend couples counseling," Cricket said. "It's important to discover differences between people that can put stress on their marriage later."

"Sometimes people just look for differences," he said. "This is one of those times."

"No, really," Cricket said. "I don't imagine raising three children is going to be any easier than what Priscilla and Pete are going through right now with their four."

"This isn't a romantic topic," Jack said. "Let's talk about how much fun last night was."

"Jack!" Cricket exclaimed, beginning to see a chink in the sexy cowboy's armor she wasn't certain she particularly liked. "This is a serious topic to me."

"Me, too. Rodeo is part of who I am. I can take a sabbatical for a few months, if you want, but—"

"And I might never stand at an altar with you," Cricket said stubbornly. "If my husband is going to be footloose and fancy free, I'd be better off learning to cope by myself."

He cheered up. "That might make you better off in Union Junction where you'd have plenty of help."

"I have parents and a brother here," she reminded him.

"That's right. I need to swing by and introduce myself to them."

"Not yet," Cricket said. "I'll let you know when I'm ready."

He didn't like the sound of that. "Cricket, while you claim that I'm the footloose one, you're awfully hard to tie down for a woman. You're supposed to jump at the chance to be a Mrs. All women do."

She winced. "Jack, sometimes you sound remarkably like your father."

"I'll take that as a compliment. Now," Jack said, "I can make you a solemn vow that I'll be very, very careful when I ride."

"Did I ever tell you that one of my favorite sports is parachuting?" Cricket asked.

"I doubt that," Jack said. "You're more a feet-on-the-ground kind of girl." How cute of her to try to rattle his cage.

"I'm most serious."

"Cricket, you don't have to try to show me how you feel. I understand that Pop has probably scared you silly about rodeo. But I assure you that the stories you hear about cowboys getting hurt, and cowboys getting nursed back to health by beautiful, sexy, willing women, are just legends we spin to each other."

She turned to stare at him. "Jack Morgan!"

He laughed. "Just kidding."

She shook her head. "I'm not."

"I know." He sighed. "Let's chalk this up as a loaded topic in our marriage."

"No," Cricket said. "I'm not kidding about parachuting. My brother is a professional parachutist. I've jumped ten times."

Something lurched inside Jack. Maybe she wasn't bluffing. Did preacher women fib like other women sometimes did, tell little white lies to get their way? He wasn't certain if he should try to call her bluff or not. She had a look in her eyes that made him wary—something that looked like calm truthfulness. He'd met a lot of fibbers in his life, and he was pretty certain Cricket wasn't bluffing. Could he have the bad fortune to fall for the one woman who liked jumping out of planes but wouldn't jump at a wedding ring? "Does Pop know this?"

"No."

"Does anyone know this about you?"

"Priscilla does."

"Well, it has to stop," Jack said, "if you're being one hundred percent honest. I don't need to be married to a parachuting preacher."

Cricket laughed. "That's what Priscilla calls me. I was a deacon, Jack, not a preacher. It's different."

He frowned. "Not to me. It means I'd be the one praying, and waiting for you to splat on the ground. Let's have no more of that silly talk."

She stopped the car in front of the doctor's office and got out. He followed, realizing she hadn't said she would obey his wishes. "Cricket, if you're pulling my leg, I don't like it."

"Okay," she said airily, and went inside the doctor's office to check herself in.

He felt himself getting a bit hot under the proverbial collar. "I'm sure your parents would never allow their only daughter to do such a thing."

"Daughter and son," Cricket said. "And we all jump together, rodeo man."

"This does not bode well for family gatherings."

"Parachuting is a lot safer than rodeo, I'll bet." Nodding to everyone in the waiting room, Cricket sat down and picked up a magazine. He glanced around at all the other pregnant women, realizing with some discomfort that he looked a lot like the other husbands in attendance. *We all look as if we'd rather be in a bar drinking a beer,* Jack thought wildly. *But I bet none of their wives jump out of planes!*

That was the problem—Cricket wasn't his wife yet, so she didn't have to obey him. He tried to reassure himself that getting married would change things. Plus, surely being a mother would give her the perspective that she needed to be safe for the sake of his children. "I'd just like to say that parachuting is from several thousand feet up," Jack said, staying on his point, "and riding a bull only takes you about eight feet off the ground, approximately."

"It's still probably safer," Cricket said serenely, apparently determined to ignore his good advice.

Jack thought the conversation had gotten way out of control. He was not happy with his pregnant fiancée at the moment. She was trying to be the one who wore the pants in their marriage, and he needed to make certain she knew right here and now that he wasn't going to put up with that. "Do any of your wives parachute?" he asked the men in the room.

Five of six masculine hands went up. Jack's jaw sagged. "Why?" he asked.

"It's fun," one of the wives told him. "Hello, Deacon Cricket," she said. "Is this the hot cowboy you've told us so much about?"

Hot cowboy? Did Cricket really think he was hot? He sneaked a peek at her to get her reaction, noting Cricket's blush. He practically puffed out his chest, recognizing guilt written all over the pretty deacon's face.

"This is Jack Morgan of Union Junction," Cricket said, ignoring the "hot cowboy" comment. "He's having a wee chicken moment about jumping."

"Oh, Mr. Morgan," another wife said, "we have quite the parachuting club in Fort Wylie. There's a small airport here. It's great fun. You'll be ever so proud when Cricket starts taking your little ones out for their first jumps."

Jack felt strange wind whirring around his ears and the next time thing he knew, he was staring up into the face of a worried nurse. Cricket was peering down at him, as well. Considering he was flat on his back, he didn't feel very soothed. "I'm afraid of heights. Nothing higher than the back of a bull for me," he told the nurse, and she nodded.

"It's okay," she said. "You'll get over that fear the first time you jump, Mr. Morgan."

Chapter Twelve

Jack wasn't feeling any better by the time Cricket went in for her appointment. The physician seemed competent, but he had a hundred questions and felt silly asking everything he felt he needed to know. So he abstained, assigning himself the role of interested listener.

"I assume it's still okay to have sexual relations?" Cricket asked, and Jack perked up. This was a question to which he very much wanted to hear a positive response.

"As long as you feel like it," Dr. Suzanne said, music to Jack's grateful ears. "At least to a certain point," the doctor qualified. She measured Cricket's stomach, the same tummy that Jack had taken his time kissing last night. He noted that it was a very shapely tummy, almost enough to give him sexual thoughts he didn't need to have at the moment. He shifted in his chair, and the doctor smiled at him.

"Don't worry," she told him, "a lot of fathers have fears about hurting their partners during intercourse.

And some worry that the baby will grab them," she said, laughing. "So please feel free to ask any questions you want to, Mr. Morgan."

Grab him? He blinked. What a horrible thing to say to a man! It was almost guaranteed to make a man anxious about things that weren't worth worrying about. "I don't have any questions," he said firmly.

She looked at Cricket. "Are you tired?"

"Just a little."

"Taking your prenatal vitamins?"

Cricket nodded. He made a mental note to make certain she was getting enough rest and taking her vitamins.

"Still nauseated?"

"It's getting better," Cricket said. "I think."

The doctor smiled. "Good." She rubbed some clear stuff on Cricket's stomach and touched a wand there. "Mr. Morgan, say hello to your children."

Like magic, he saw waves and curves on the screen. He saw a lot of black and white but nothing that looked as much like babies. Still, he fancied he could see something. "Are there really three?"

"It's quite a jumble in there," the doctor explained. "But they seem content for the moment."

"Can you tell how big they are? Can you estimate how long I have before I'll need full bed rest?" Cricket asked.

"Considering your size, I don't expect you to go past October, Maybe November. We'll do what we can to keep them inside you and growing healthfully as long as possible."

Jack blinked. October! That didn't give him a lot of

time to get Cricket to the altar. He needed to get his father out of the hospital and on his feet. Laura was due with her baby any day. He swallowed, realizing that if he was going to convince Cricket to marry him, he needed to do it quickly, because she wasn't likely to feel the same need after the babies were born. He'd seen the slight embarrassment on her face in the waiting room; he'd known what she was thinking: *Here sits Deacon Cricket, local good girl gone bad.*

Those were *his* babies in her belly—he had to help her see the urgency of the matter. There was a lot that needed to be settled between them. The whole parachuting thing had thrown him. Frankly, he and Cricket needed to start developing a relationship where he would have some say in her life. If they weren't married, Cricket might begrudgingly label him a friend and nothing more.

"You're very quiet over there, Mr. Morgan," the doctor said, and Jack swallowed. Cricket looked at him with big brown eyes.

He needed to say something appropriate to the moment. But he was so lost.

"I'm gonna be a dad," he said slowly, wondering if he'd be any better at it than his father.

Could he be?

"CRICKET, I NEED TO MEET your parents. And your brother. Soon, like today."

"Don't you think you should go home and see your father? He's recuperating from major surgery."

"Pop's got an army of people taking care of him. He'll appreciate my desire to introduce myself to your family."

"They're still digesting the fact of my pregnancy," she said. "I was slow to confess my situation." Truthfully she hadn't confessed it at all—yet. In fact, she was still deciding how to best tell them. She didn't have a lot of time before the Fort Wylie grapevine got to them, but still, Cricket didn't want Jack to know she was reluctant to disappoint her parents.

"I'd really like to meet them," he said, and Cricket sighed.

"I should warn you that they may not welcome you with open arms."

"I suppose that's fair," he said. "They looked forward to better for their daughter?" He wanted to know what he was in for, felt some determination to make things right in his life, at least do a better job with her family than he'd done with his own. "Did they feel that you'd been swept off your feet by a man who had no potential and no intention of settling down?"

"Well, I wouldn't—"

"Then they were right." Jack took her keys, opened the passenger-side door for her. "No more driving for you, Deacon. It's rest from now on. I don't want you lifting your littlest finger. I will take care of everything, just like Dr. Suzanne said."

"Jack!" Cricket hung back, refusing to sit down. "The doctor didn't say I was on bed rest yet."

"*I* say you're on bed rest. I intend to carry you and my babies around on a pillow."

"No," Cricket said stubbornly. "I don't want that. I'm used to being independent."

"Me, too," Jack said, "but I'm changing."

"No, you're not. You're exactly the same person who jumped into my car in January. You're avoiding your own family by focusing on me and mine."

"You need me more than they do," he pointed out. "Call your parents and ask them if they feel like meeting your Prince Charming."

Cricket shook her head. "Prince Charmings aren't supposed to be so bossy. And can you let the clutch out gently? This is a vintage Bug and I intend to keep it forever."

He looked at the floorboard and then the long stick shift. "Cricket," he said, "I hate this car."

She smiled and shrugged. "You don't like a lot about me, cowboy."

"No, I'm serious. This isn't a car, it's a tin can. I feel like I'm in the Flintstonemobile."

She looked at him, one eyebrow raised knowingly. "Can't drive a stick?"

No man liked to be caught looking inadequate, especially when he was applying for the role of chief protector in his lady's life. "Only in an emergency, and only if the vehicle isn't ancient. Where did you get this 'vintage' car?"

"My father won it years ago in a raffle." She gave him an airy glance. "My brother, Thad, keeps my car running for me. I can teach you how to drive it."

He wasn't sure he wanted to be taught anything by

a woman who was pregnant with his triplets. Shouldn't he be taking care of her? "I'm going to buy you a minivan. That will solve everything. Where's the nearest dealership?"

He meant it. Today he was going to buy her the safest, biggest minivan on the market, complete with OnStar in case she got lost between here and Union Junction.

Cricket's lips pinched. Her pretty, brown eyes narrowed. With some trepidation, Jack recognized a storm brewing. "Is there a problem, little mama?"

"Yes," she said. "You. Get out of my car, you stubborn ape."

CRICKET LEFT JACK standing on the pavement in front of the doctor's office. The man could just find his own way home. He had plenty to deal with in his own house—he could just quit worrying about her. "My children, my car, my family," she muttered, motoring away from the cowboy. "My hobbies, my business, my pregnancy."

That was the problem. He wanted to worry about everything about her—he wanted to take over her life.

She liked her life just the way it was, thank you.

He said she was stubborn.

What she was was a shade dishonest.

She hadn't told her parents about the babies, and she hadn't mentioned she'd quit her job. In short, she couldn't take Jack home to her parents. Ultimately, she was worse about dealing with family matters than he was.

All the time she'd been trying to get him to tend to Josiah, she'd really been avoiding him getting to know her own family. "Where's an unmarried and pregnant gal's fairy godmother when she needs one?" she asked, and decided it was time to face life without one.

CRICKET PRESSED IN the numbers on the electronic keypad, and drove through when the massive wrought-iron gates parted. She rang the doorbell, her heartbeat suddenly racing. This visit was long past due.

"Cricket," her mother said, "how nice to see you."

"Hello, Mother."

She stepped into the highly polished marble foyer, waiting for her father to appear.

"Reed, Cricket's come to pay us a visit."

"Excellent, Eileen," her father said. "Cricket, dear, we've been expecting you."

Of course they were. By now they'd probably had fifty phone calls updating them on her downfall. Cricket sighed. "I've been trying to work things out on my own."

"I suspected as much," her mother said. "We wish you didn't have such an independent streak, dear. Your father and I hate standing on the sidelines when we wish we could help you."

Cricket followed her parents into the palatial living room, taking a seat near the huge bay window. "Everyone wants to help me," she said. "I feel a great need to stand on my own two feet."

Eileen blinked. "We know. That's why we didn't call."

Cricket glanced around. "Where's Thad?"

"Your brother is playing polo at the club. He told us you resigned from the church." Eileen looked sorry about that. "Cricket, dear, we know that working in the church was your dream."

"I've had a lot of dreams that haven't worked out," Cricket said. "I seem to be a bit unfocused these days."

"Well," Reed said, "entrepreneurs don't always hit the right note the first time out."

"That's the problem," Cricket said. "I'm not an entrepreneur. I was a deacon. But then, I fell for an inappropriate man, a man I knew wasn't right for me, who is the furthest thing from stable that he could ever be. The only thing I ever did that was stable was the Lord's work," Cricket said. "And now I'm pregnant and unmarried. How's that for not exactly practicing what I preach?"

"Oh, dear," Eileen said. "Reed, did Cricket just say we're going to be grandparents?" She fanned herself, looking faint.

Reed patted his wife's hand. "We hadn't heard *that* piece of news, Cricket." He looked as if he didn't know what to say.

"I just told the father and his family yesterday." Cricket felt small and selfish for visiting this shock on her parents. "I've really made a mess of things."

"Now, listen," her mother said, sitting up and accepting a glass of whiskey from her husband, "babies are not messy."

"No, but the parents are. At least these babies' parents are."

"Babies?" Eileen repeated, her voice very faint.

Cricket nodded. "I'm having triplets."

Eileen and Reed stared at their only daughter, their faces frozen.

"My goodness," Eileen said after a moment, "your cowboy must be in shock."

"I'll say," Reed said. "Three children and a wife will certainly cut into his winnings."

Cricket's mind was made up for her with that comment. "I'm not about to be a burden."

"What do you mean?" Eileen asked.

"I'm going to raise these children on my own." Cricket nodded, feeling all the pressure fall away from her. "Single motherhood, the most independent thing a woman can do."

"I'll say," her father said. "Ever changed a diaper?"

"Some," Cricket said, but now that she'd made her decision, she knew she was right. With the power of prayer and maybe a dozen child-rearing books, she could give being a mother her very best effort.

Independence was the only reason she hadn't accepted Jack's offer of marriage. Otherwise she'd always wonder if that footloose cowboy had proposed because he'd had to; she'd always wonder if she'd said yes because she was too afraid of standing on her own two feet when faced with three pairs of tiny eyes trusting her to do everything right.

Chapter Thirteen

Jack wanted to stay in Fort Wylie and wait for Cricket to return—he was hanging out in his truck parked at her house/tea shop—but the call he got from Pete changed his mind.

"Laura's gone into labor," Pete said.

"I'll be right there."

It didn't feel right leaving Cricket, even though she'd been annoyed with him when she'd driven off. Petty annoyances passed, didn't they? Hopefully she wasn't the kind of girl who stayed mad. The only way he knew to work the kink out of an angry female was by making love to her, whispering soft apologies. Cricket didn't strike him as the kind of woman who'd settle for that.

But he could hope.

He scribbled a note and left it on her door so she'd know Laura and Gabe's baby was on the way.

By the time he got to Union Junction and the hospital, the baby had been born. "Go on in and see her," Dane told him with a grin. "Gabe's got him a cute little girl."

"A girl?" A girl to go with Penny and Perrin.

"Perrin'll be caught between two girls," Gabe said.

"That could be a good thing or a bad thing," Jack replied.

Gabe laughed. "Only time will tell."

Jack had grabbed some flowers and a pink giraffe in the hospital's gift shop. He walked into Laura's room holding the flowers aloft like an awkward prize. "How's the new mother?" he asked, handing the flowers to Laura as he gave her a kiss on the cheek and Gabe a slap on the back.

"Fine." Laura looked tired but happy. "This is Gabriella Michele. Gabriella, meet your uncle Jack."

Jack glanced at the baby with some fear, not daring to touch her. She seemed so tiny and peaceful snuggling in the crook of her mother's arm. "She's beautiful."

Laura smiled. "Gabe and I are hoping you'll be her godfather."

Jack glanced up, stunned. "Godfather?" His only recollection of a godfather was from the movies. What was expected of a real-life godfather?

Gabe laughed. "Yes. Laura and I decided it was time to tie you into the family."

Jack glanced again at the small, pink-wrapped bundle. "Are you sure?"

"Yes. Godfather Jack," Laura said, teasing. "You'll be the best. And it will give you practice."

He looked up at his brother and his wife. "I'll need lots of it."

Gabe laughed. "You'll get up to speed on babies very quickly."

Jack shook his head. "Life's moving very quickly on me, almost conspiracy-like."

"Have you told Pop about the triplets?" Gabe asked.

"I haven't even seen him. I came right here."

Laura smiled. "I think he wants to talk to you."

Jack felt guilty he hadn't hung around to see his father come out of surgery. "How's he doing?"

"Really, really well," Laura said. "But he's been asking for you. Bellowing for you, actually."

"Guess I'll step around to see him." Jack didn't feel particularly excited at the thought, but he also knew he couldn't put it off any longer.

"Are you going to do it?" Gabe asked curiously.

Jack knew exactly what his brother was asking. "What, move to the ranch?"

Gabe shrugged. "Just a warning, Pop's sure he's been warned by spirits that you have no intention of moving to the ranch because Mom's there."

Well, that was certainly odd. But Gabe could have no idea how correct Pop's "spirits" were. The old man was eerily prescient. "Hey, let me just celebrate being Godfather Jack for now, okay?"

"And Papa Jack," Laura said.

"That, too. Later on I'll worry about being Good Son Jack."

"And Millionaire Jack," Gabe reminded him. "The only way to the grail is through Mom this time."

"Yeah, well, who needs money, anyway?" Jack asked, and Gabe and Laura laughed.

"A man who's having triplets," Gabe called after him. "College educations and weddings are expensive."

Jack headed down the hall. "Hey, Pop," he said, entering his father's room.

Suzy and Dane were keeping Josiah company, but they got up and quietly exited when Jack walked in. "He's been asking for you," Dane said as he walked by.

Pop's eyes opened. "Jack?"

"Yeah, Pop. It's me. How are you feeling?"

"Probably the best I can feel after Dr. Moneybags has poked around inside me." He glanced up. "Where the hell did you go?"

Jack sat down next to his father. "I had to go see Cricket."

"Why isn't she here?" Josiah demanded.

"She had some things to do back in Fort Wylie." Jack patted his father's arm. "She's going to be busy now that's she's having triplets."

"Triplets?" Josiah's eyebrows raised. "Whoa," he said, "you knocked that ball out of the park, son!"

Jack shook his head. "When do you get out of here?"

"I don't know." Pop glanced around him weakly. "But when I do, I'm marrying Sara."

"Good for you." Jack was genuinely glad for his father.

"Let's make it a double," Pop suggested.

"My lady won't have me. Yet." Jack leaned back in the chair. "She's got a lot on her mind."

"Hmm." Josiah grinned. "*Triplets*. They'll sure keep

you busy. Better get Cricket convinced to marry you before they're born, because she'll think of a hundred excuses afterward not to do it. She's still got pregnancy weight and won't look good in a wedding gown, that's one excuse. Or she'll say that she can't leave the children to go on a honeymoon. Or if you wait just a few years, the kids can be in the wedding." Pop looked at him. "Believe me, if the babies come before the ring, you're in for what is known as a prolonged engagement."

Jack's throat went dry. Pop's words seemed like good advice. "It does sound like something Cricket would do," he said slowly, realizing that if she was reluctant now, she wasn't going to become any more eager. "She's not the most conventional woman."

Josiah chuckled. "You wouldn't have wanted a conventional woman."

"I suppose not," Jack said, uncertain. He would have at least liked the woman he chose to be more excited about being his wife. "Hey, congratulations, Pop, on finding a good woman."

"I found two good women," Josiah said, "and I don't intend to make the same mistakes with the second one that I made with the first. Fortunately for me, the first one has forgiven me. Which reminds me, when are you going to do some forgiving of your own?"

Jack winced. "I've forgiven you, Pop."

"I don't need your forgiveness!" Josiah stated. "I meant your mother!"

Jack shrugged. "I'm not sure what to forgive."

"Well, you better figure it out," Pop said, "because as far as I can tell, you've got three babies on the way and a woman who doesn't want to marry you—two strikes against you—and you don't seem to have moved your things to the ranch." Josiah sniffed. "If I were a betting man—and I am—I'd bet your million dollars is going to stay safely in my wallet."

Jack wondered how much more a man had to be willing to give of himself besides a kidney to get a little peace. But with Josiah Morgan, Jack knew peace was a long way off.

JACK HAD a weighty decision to make. He was a god-father now, and that gave him a new look into the life of a man responsible for a child. He wanted to be a good godfather and a good parent, and the one thing that was staring him in the face was his lifestyle and lack of a secure income.

As his brothers were quick to point out, babies were expensive.

He knew Cricket well enough to know that she was going to try to raise three children and run the tea shop to pay her bills. Maybe she'd meant to purchase the tea shop and have someone else run it as an investment, but he doubted that. Cricket was an independent woman; she'd want to be involved in everything. She said she'd quit her job because of her unwed-and-pregnant status, but the ladies in the waiting room of Dr. Suzanne's office hadn't seemed cool to her at all. In fact, they'd seemed quite warm and friendly. He wondered if

Cricket had made a decision she'd regret by resigning from her deacon's position, then decided it was none of his business for the moment.

What he had to decide was how he intended to convince her that he had the ability to take care of her.

The easiest way to financial stability was to do as Pop asked, blast him, which was exactly what had hung up his brothers. However, they hadn't wanted to get married—not at first—and he did, pronto.

It was a weird thought. He was begging to be a family man, and he couldn't get his lady to have him.

His cell phone rang, and to his surprise he saw it was Cricket. His heartbeat sped up. "Hello?"

"Jack, it's Cricket."

"How are you?"

"I'm fine. Listen," she said, "I apologize for ditching you this morning."

"I know you've got a lot on your mind. I shouldn't have teased you about your car." He mentally slapped himself, thinking it was a subject best left alone, like the parachuting. She'd come to her senses about jumping out of high-flying vehicles when the babies were born. Three small infants would settle her down.

"Jack," Cricket said, "I just want you to know that I think it's best if we don't see each other for a while."

His heart crashed. "Why?"

"I…I'm just not comfortable," she explained. "I need to figure some things out on my own. When you're around, I catch myself falling into a pattern of convenience."

He frowned. "What the hell is a pattern of convenience?"

"Something I don't want. When you're around, you take over. And I seem to let you."

"Yeah, well," Jack said, not sure that he agreed that she let him do anything, "I think you should just marry me and be an independent wife."

"Jack, I can't marry you. It would be a mistake. The fundamental differences in our lifestyles would eventually catch up with us."

She meant rodeo. She envisioned herself as a rodeo widow. He shook his head. If that's what this all came down to, he supposed he'd have to concede the point. "I've got to make a living."

"I understand."

He didn't think she did, especially when he couldn't say, "Hey, let's compromise, no rodeo for me, no parachuting for you," because he knew very well she'd blast his ears for trying to tie her down. It stunk being the one who was trying to do the tying down. "Cricket," he said, "I'm trying really hard to change."

"I don't want you to change," Cricket said. "I think things that are wild should be left to the wild."

"Well, I'm getting tamer all the time, Deacon. I'm a godfather now."

"To Laura's baby? Did she have her baby?"

"Yes. A healthy baby girl named Gabriella Michele. And I'm pretty darn excited about being a god-pop."

"That's great, Jack."

She didn't sound like she much cared. "Hey, Pop was asking about you."

"I hope he's doing well," she said quickly. "Will you please tell him I won't be able to do those drapes like I promised? I'm sure your mother would probably prefer to select her own, anyway."

Curtains were just the cover for what she was really trying to say. He sensed her slipping away from him. He knew the sound of someone escaping—he'd done it often enough to know. "Cricket—"

"I have to go, Jack," she said, and he heard the inevitable *thanks for the memories* in her voice.

"Cricket, dammit," he began, but the phone went dead. "That conversation went nowhere," he muttered. Didn't she care that she was shredding his heart? He wanted to be with her—he was darn sure they belonged together!

She didn't think so. And she was holding all the aces.

He had no choice but to try to convince that stubborn woman he was serious about being a family man.

His phone buzzed, alerting him that he had a text.

Just heard that you're expecting some ankle-biters, he read. Congratulations, you ol' dog.

He snorted at the words from a good rodeo buddy.

Another buzz.

Three children for the man who always said he'd never be a father? Way to ride!

Jack sighed. It was true—he'd certainly won the prize for fastest ride to fatherhood.

The texts kept rolling in. His spirits sank a bit as he

received blessings and well wishes from his rodeo family. His worlds were colliding, shifting.

Which was exactly what he knew was bugging Cricket—she didn't want to change him. She didn't want to be responsible for him having to change.

Change was going to happen to both of them eventually. On whose terms, he wasn't certain.

For now, he turned his truck toward the Morgan ranch.

Chapter Fourteen

Jack walked inside the house on the Morgan ranch, stunned to find his mother in the kitchen making cookies. He cleared his throat. "Hi."

She turned, smiling when she saw him. *"Bonjour!"*

He was uncomfortable with finding her in the house, much more than he'd thought he'd be.

"Moving in?" Gisella asked.

"I guess so."

She began rolling dough. "I'm glad you're here. Your father needs to lose his bet."

He blinked. Was that a friendly comment, or was she being antagonistic toward Josiah? "Why do you say that?"

She shrugged. "He wants to. He likes to think he's moving all of us around. Josiah is a stubborn man."

He sat at the kitchen table, deciding that maybe it was time they had this conversation. "What's in it for you?"

"Me?" She glanced at him. "My kids." She bobbed

her head up and down. "And I'll have to admit, I've long wanted a second chance with Josiah."

Jack frowned. "He's planning to marry Sara, you know."

"Oh, I didn't mean that kind of second chance. I like Sara. I'm glad they're getting married!" She washed her hands as she finished placing dough balls on the cookie sheet. "But I never felt good about leaving Josiah the way I did. So I jumped at the chance to come back on different terms than we had before."

He was starting to get the picture. "You want redemption."

"Of course I do. Don't you?" She looked at him curiously.

He didn't know if he could forgive this stranger standing in the kitchen enough to forget all the years he'd wondered why she left. "I'm sure I do," he said carefully, knowing he was in much the same position as his mother, "but it goes both ways."

"I can do no more than hope for reconciliation. I can't change the past."

He didn't say anything, his silence an acknowledgment of her hopes. She was being very brave about returning home to a family she didn't know, and he realized he couldn't quite say the same about himself.

"I'm going to make the guesthouse my home," she said. "You'll be able to live here, if you want to."

"You don't have to do that," he said quickly. "In fact, Cricket's leaving the draperies and doodads to you. This is your home."

She shook her head. "The guesthouse is more space than I need. You, on the other hand, have a growing family. Unless you're planning on living in Fort Wylie."

"I don't know what I'm planning." Would Cricket move into this house with him when she had the babies? He didn't think she'd want to leave her mother, father, brother. Her tea shop. Her friends. He'd move there in a snap, but he didn't think Cricket would welcome that. Hadn't she just told him to shove off, in so many words? "I'm not planning anything," he said, "because the mother of my children seems to think she should raise our children on her own."

Gisella looked at him curiously. "I doubt she intends to keep you from your children."

"No, but she doesn't intend for me to live under a roof with her, either." Why was he telling his mother this? He hadn't planned to. It felt strange, out of place. And yet somehow comforting.

"It's a difficult thing you're both trying to do." Gisella put some baked cookies onto a plate, then took some flour out of the cupboard. "Let me make you a crepe."

"A crepe?" Was that the French version of comfort food? "You don't have to do that," he said, stiffening against the idea of her trying to mother him. The time for that was long past. "Thanks, though."

"A little powdered sugar," she murmured, looking around in the cupboard. "Simple food, you know. When you were a boy, you loved my crepes."

He frowned. "I don't remember."

"Of course you do not. It was a very long time ago. Still, I remember."

He suddenly realized how hard it had been on his mother to live with the memories of them growing up. She alone had held her memories, knowing that her children would not remember her, not much about her, anyway. He remembered some vague things, a flash of memory here, a sliver of laughter there.

"Look," she said with delight, "my old crepe pan!"

She held up a small copper pan, her face joyful. It wasn't gleaming—he doubted anyone had polished— or used it—in years. A slight smile twisted his lips. He watched her look at the pan with delight, as if she remembered all the times she'd used it fondly, and sudden bittersweet nostalgia overwhelmed him. He had loved his mother. He had missed her fiercely.

He got up and enveloped her in his arms, giving her the embrace he should have given her when she'd returned. "I've missed you," he said suddenly against the ache, and she laid her head against his chest for just a moment.

"When I left, I was taller than you," she said. "You were a little boy, only eight years old. Now you are so much taller than me."

"It's all right," he said, feeling her pained sadness in her thin shoulders, even the bones in her back, as she seemed resigned to the dark-shadowed memories. "You're home now."

"But I'm not forgiven," she murmured.

He said, "You are by me, Mother," and then he held

her as she wept the same tears he knew he would one day if he wasn't there every moment for his babies' tears, their laughter, their falls and their eventual flights from his own nest.

SETTLING AT THE RANCH was part of the bargain, and now that Jack had chosen his course, he was determined to do it well. He moved into the main house as his mother had suggested, then arranged a meeting with his brothers to discuss the best options for making a living.

"I don't have a whole lot of time," he said to Dane, Pete and Gabe as they all sat in the den of the home Josiah had envisioned as the place where the brothers would one day forge familial bonds. It hadn't happened, not the way their father had hoped, anyway, and yet still Jack felt closer to his brothers than he had in years.

"Hell, you'll think you have no time once those babies of yours are born," Pete told him. "You're still a bachelor right now with time to spare. We're the ones with no time."

"Sorry," Jack said gruffly, handing out beers. "I didn't mean my time was short today. I meant that Cricket's going to give birth, and I need to make some viable plans for the old bank account."

Dane grinned. "It's kind of funny to hear you talking like a family man."

Jack grunted. "Laugh all you like. The gods are laughing, too. But I still need to figure out my finances. I didn't know if you guys were interested in doing anything around here."

"Gisella owns the place now," Gabe reminded him.

Jack nodded. "She gave us the free and clear to make the property our own. She said she'd like to see it become a useful and lively place. Apparently, her parents baked pies and grew vines for homemade wine, so she believes land should stay busy and productive."

Pete looked at him. "We never met our grandparents. Are they still alive?"

"I don't know." Nobody knew much about Gisella's family. "Guess you could ask her. And I suppose one day we should open up Pandora's box and read the letters she sent us over the years." Jack frowned. "Not that I'm eager, but I sort of feel like we owe it to her."

He felt a little sadder than he expected to over his father's confession about the letters. All the years he'd believed his mother hadn't cared enough to write, cared enough to remember them…him.

"I'm sort of surprised she'd care to return after what he did to her. It takes an awful lot of forgiveness to love someone who sabotages your relationship with your children," Gabe said.

They digested that silently. Her return was too new for any of them to start examining the family tree. Jack certainly didn't want to stir up anything that might be painful to her. "Maybe she came back here because she had no one left in France."

Dane shrugged. "Possibly. Anyway, baking's not a bad idea, but none of us bake anything anybody would want, and vines take time and water and real experience that none of us have. We should probably stick to live-stock, which we do know something about, if we're going to pick a family brand."

"I heard some of you were thinking about breeding horses," Jack said.

Gabe said, "I assume you need fast income."

"True," Jack said. "My window of opportunity is somewhat shorter than it used to be."

"There's all those pecan trees," Dane said thought-fully.

"Yeah," Jack said. "That's right."

They sat silently, sipping their beers.

"The obvious answer might be to open a dude ranch, or even a bed-and-breakfast," Pete said. "But I don't know if I've got the stomach for strangers."

"Or the time," Gabe said.

"Cricket parachutes," Jack said, feeling the sudden need to have some sympathy from his brothers.

"No," Pete said. "If we bring a business like that out here, the liability would be insane."

Jack blinked. His brothers didn't seem surprised by his announcement at all. Why did he have to be the only one bothered by his woman's penchant for danger? "All I know is rodeo."

"Here's a stupid idea," Gabe said. "What about a haunted house?"

His brothers stared at him, their jaws slack for an instant.

"Why don't we just go all the way and open up an alien-sighting tourist attraction?" Pete asked, his tone ironic. "Or a circus. We've got enough sideshows in this family."

"Go ahead," Dane said crossly, "we'll just finally confirm to everyone in Union Junction that we're all crazy as goats around here."

"I *said* it was a crazy idea," Gabe said, "but at least I threw out a suggestion. What have you guys got?"

"Okay," Jack said, deciding to intervene before tempers flared. "Brainstorming's good. We need something that's—"

"Making money hand over fist doesn't seem to come easy to us," Gabe said. "Maybe Pop didn't pass his golden touch along to us."

They sat silently, considering the fact that maybe Pop was the only one among them who knew how to turn dirt into gold. "We haven't had any practice," Jack said. "This is the first time we've ever tried to come up with a creative plan for fiscal benefit."

"Which is scary when you consider that there are four of us trying to figure it out, and Pop did it on his own with four kids," Dane said, not pleased. "Pete, you have an excuse if your brain is mush with four infants keeping you up at night, but the rest of us should be pretty sharp."

Jack thought about his three on the way. He had to prove to Cricket that he was more than capable of being a good provider. "Who wants another beer?"

Without waiting for an answer, Jack got up and grabbed three more cans from the fridge, and another Coke for himself, and passed them around to his brothers. "Hell, I don't even know where I'm going to live. No wonder I can't figure out what business I should run."

Pete raised his brows. "You haven't talked Cricket into moving to Union Junction?"

"She doesn't want to leave her tea shop," Jack told him. "She plans to open it soon, and said one of us needs to have steady employment."

"Ouch," Dane said.

"Yeah," Jack said. "And she's got her family and friends there. She quit her church post, but I'm not sure if that will stick. Her doctor is there. All in all, I haven't been able to figure out a compelling reason to ask her to leave Fort Wylie."

"You're not compelling enough?" Gabe asked, and his brothers grinned.

"And she hasn't invited you to move in with her," Dane said, to which Jack shrugged.

"She's more practical than I, and pointed out that I'd forfeit a million dollars if I did move there. I'm only now beginning to process calling Pop on his bet. He thinks I have no plans to move to the ranch because of Mom. It's important to prove the old badger wrong." He leaned back in the chair, letting the leather of his father's recliner suck him into its comfort. "Mom and I have been talking, so on that front improvement's being made. The four of us are sitting here together, so improvement's happening family-wise, just like Pop wanted. But Cricket says she doesn't want to see me for a while," he admitted, his body sagging with defeat.

"So I'm back to square one there. I'm just trying to make something of myself so she'll want me."

"It's not your finances holding you back," Pete said. "Cricket's not that shallow. It has to be something else."

"She says I overwhelm her," Jack told his brothers. "She says she's not as independent when I'm around. I think she's annoyed that I won't quit rodeo when I insisted she give up jumping out of planes. We're sort of at an impasse."

Silence met his words. Jack wondered what Cricket was doing right now. "I think I'll head to Fort Wylie. Maybe a bright idea will hit me on the way there."

"Thought you said Cricket doesn't want to see you for a while," Dane said.

Jack stood. "Simple miscommunication," he said. "If I can fix things around here with Pop, Mom and you guys, surely I can fix my relationship with a deacon."

"Forgiveness is easier to give than to get," Gabe said.

"What dummy said that? It's terrible advice," Jack told him, and Gabe shrugged. "If we all believed that," Jack continued, "we'd all be in a sinking boat. Anyway, I can't think about Pop right now. I need to meet Cricket's family. I need to figure out my woman, whether she likes it or not. Then I'll come up with a big idea for employment."

"That's the man," Pete said jovially. "Action instead of moping."

"Moping?" Jack repeated.

"I meant sitting around thinking," Pete explained

hurriedly. He raised his beer can in Jack's direction. "Good luck and Godspeed. Let us know how it goes."

Jack stood, well aware his brothers were enjoying his dilemma with empathy and a little humor. That was okay. He knew they supported him, and it was a good feeling after all the years apart. "Hey," he said suddenly, "I never thanked you for sneaking out to see me ride. And then trying to come to the hospital. I never said it, but it scared the hell out of me when your car got hit."

Pete cleared his throat. Dane shrugged. Gabe grinned. "It was a wild night," Gabe said. "We made Pop a tougher man than he ever dreamed he'd need to be."

They all laughed, remembering how blazing mad Pop had been. But he'd been upset that his boys were sneaking out, frightened that they'd nearly gotten killed in a car accident. Jack understood that now. Parents didn't always show their emotions the way they felt them. He hoped he'd be able to tell his kids how much he loved them, then figured he'd better give himself a pass on being the perfect parent. "It was great knowing you were there," Jack said. "I liked having the coolest cheering section around."

"You better figure out a way to get Cricket to cheer for you," Pete said, and Jack headed toward Fort Wylie.

Chapter Fifteen

This time Jack skipped Cricket's house altogether and went straight to her family home. Most likely, Cricket wouldn't be happy with this decision, but if he waited on her to introduce him, he'd be a father already. He had no intention of letting her be a single mom—he needed to get her safely to the altar without further delay. The wait was beginning to wear on him, and one thing he'd learned about the deacon. She could drag her feet like no other woman he'd ever known.

He managed to get himself buzzed through the massive wrought-iron gate by giving only his name and the nature of his call, which surprised him. He was greeted at the door of a large home—about the size of the Morgan home at the ranch, but built in a Grecian style—by an elegant, older version of Cricket, tall and dark-haired and manicured. "Mrs. Jasper?"

"Yes?" she said, giving his jeans, boots and cowboy hat a quick once-over, before her gaze peered past him to his truck for the briefest of moments.

He removed his hat. "My name is Jack Morgan."

"I've heard the name." She showed him in to a white room that was air-conditioned—or just cold from the marble—and smiled at him. "You've come about my daughter, Cricket."

He resisted the nervous feeling settling into the pit of his stomach. This was a first for him, and being on the receiving end of a mother's scrutiny was unsettling. He made a mental note to remember when his daughters— surely he would have at least one daughter in Cricket's and his batch of triplets—had sweethearts over, he would keep the air-conditioning low and his demeanor antiseptic. No sense in encouraging every Tom, Dick and Harry to date his pink-ribboned darlings—but he was no average Tom, Dick or Harry. "Yes, ma'am, I have come about Cricket."

She looked him over again, then seemed to make a decision. "Please seat yourself in the den. I will let my husband, Reed, know that you are calling." She looked down at his boots, then at her white rug—he could almost feel her suppressing a mental shiver—then seemed relieved when he said, "I'll just wait right here, ma'am."

"Please call me Eileen," she said, then drifted down the hall.

"Whoa," he murmured to himself as he watched Mrs. Jasper depart. No wonder Cricket loved her tea shop and gingerbread house. It had life and warmth— this house was a displaced part of the Arctic Circle. He was shocked when Cricket and two men came down the hall, followed by her mother.

"Jack! What are you doing here?" Cricket asked, not sounding as thrilled as he might have hoped. Still, he hadn't told her that he was coming, and she was one of those independent women who thought they had to be in control of everything. This time, he was going to be in control, he thought, right before he found himself lying on the floor, staring up at the ceiling. *This seems to happen a lot around Cricket,* he thought, noting the blue frescoes on the ceiling surrounding the chandelier and the throbbing in his jaw.

"Thad!" Cricket hurried to help Jack up. "Why did you do that?"

Jack wondered the same, but he also knew. In fact, he completely understood her brother's reaction. "It's all right," he said gamely, sitting up. "I'm fine." He pushed Cricket's hands away from him and got to his feet. "You only get one shot at me, buster, and I figure I had that one coming." He glared at Cricket's brother and father. "Be warned, next time I will send your ass into the next county."

"Oh, dear," Eileen said. "Gentlemen, let's not fight. I'm sure we can solve this problem without violence."

"Mother!" Cricket exclaimed. "There is no problem! Thad, if you do anything like that again, you'll not be an uncle to my babies! Come on, Jack," she said, pulling him into the white room despite his boots. "Sit down."

"Don't coddle me," he said impatiently. "I've been thrown from small bulls that did more damage than your brother did." He raised his chin at the other males in the room, deciding to simply skip the niceties altogether. "I came to introduce myself. We've met, and clearly we won't be sharing a table at the holidays, which is fine by me." He stared at each of them before placing his hat back on his head. "Thank you for your hospitality. I'll see myself out."

"Jack!" Cricket said, following him down the hall. "Be reasonable."

He didn't answer, just kept walking. He'd been through a lot for this woman, but he wasn't going to be told to be reasonable or any other silliness. She'd put him on hold, she'd run off on him, she'd given him the silent treatment, all of which he'd been very patient with.

If Cricket wanted him, she knew where to find him.

TIME HAD NEVER CREPT so slowly for Jack. By mid-June, Jack knew Cricket wasn't going to look him up. By July, he knew she had no plans at all to even spare him a phone call. By August, he was hanging on to hope only by his bare knuckles.

Even Josiah didn't ask him anymore about Cricket, nor did his brothers. Occasionally, he knew that Suzy, Laura or Priscilla went to see her in Fort Wylie, but they shared no news with him or their spouses. He wasn't sure why, but the deacon had deemed herself totally off limits, and he had to tell himself every day that he could lead a horse to water but for darn sure he couldn't make it drink, and right now, Cricket was in no mood to be led anywhere. He'd just dig himself into a deep hole with her, and that was no way to start off a parenting relationship. But waiting was the hardest thing he'd ever done by far. It was agonizing.

He worked on getting the barns pulled together. He inspected the pecan trees, wondering about harvesting them into some sort of crop. Only a few of them really needed spraying; most of them were healthy. He went and watched a rodeo in Lonely Hearts Station but didn't participate, all the will gone out of him. A man needed fire to compete, and he knew he was on a low burn for something else.

He kept Josiah company and got to know his brothers' children, the most fun he could remember having in a long time. The years seemed to melt away, for all of them. He thought he hadn't realized how much he missed them, but he knew in his heart his brothers were the only humans on earth who knew him better than he knew himself. Sometimes he wondered about all the years they'd lost, but then, he knew that everything had a purpose. So he didn't let himself think about the lost years and focused instead on the found ones.

He went down to the guesthouse every few nights and ate dinner with Gisella. The part of him that was sad that she'd left began to blossom with good thoughts and new memories. He grilled on her patio, and they sat on the wicker love seat chatting about things that mattered to no one but them. Gisella talked about her life in France, and how she'd known she would one day return home to Texas. He learned that her parents had passed away, but she still had many cousins, aunts and

uncles. She treasured the years she'd spent with her
mother and father but had sorely missed her boys. She'd
known Josiah would never let her take the boys with her
to France, and she'd known she could not stay with
Josiah.

Jack knew all too well how his father could force a
person between a rock and a hard place, with nowhere
to turn but away. The anger he'd kept burning for so
long inside him slowly banked, the fire out for good.

The only advice his mother had for him about
Cricket was to let her come to him, which is what his
father must have done concerning Gisella. Only, years
later, when Gisella had come home, they were simply
friends and nothing more, which suited everyone. Jack
had no intention of being just friends with Cricket. He
had fallen too hard for her, too much in love, to let her
turn their relationship into friendship. He'd wait—but
he also knew his waiting had a shelf life. Sooner or later,
his babies would make her call him. So he waited,
enjoying his nieces and nephews, planning a business
with his brothers, watching his father heal under Sara's
ministrations with some amazement. Josiah married
Sara one Sunday under a canopy of pecan trees, with
the setting sun behind them for decoration, and everyone threw birdseed at them and ate cake baked by Sara
herself. Cricket didn't come to the wedding, but she
sent a basket of teas and kitchen goodies, which Sara
loved because she was always baking.

Jack gritted his teeth and told himself his waiting
wasn't forever, even if it seemed as if it was.

And then suddenly, on a Monday night in late September, his cell phone rang and he saw it was Cricket. He felt his heart rate skid and then escalate like no bull riding had ever jacked his blood. "Hello?"

"Jack, it's Cricket."

"Hi," he said, putting down the sponge he'd been oiling a saddle with. "What's up?"

"I wondered if…you'd like to come visit."

Would he? This was the invitation he'd waited months to receive! "If that's what you want," he said, heading toward the barn sink to wash his hands.

"I do," she said. "And you might want to bring a change of clothes."

"Oh?" His brows raised, but he masked his surprise.

"Yes," she said, "I'm having a Cesarean section tomorrow, and I know you'll probably want to be around for the birth of your children."

He jogged toward his house. "All right," he said. "Will you be at your house or your parents'?"

"I'll be at my house," she said. "Come as soon as you can, please."

She hung up. He stared at his silent phone for a second, then snapped it off. "Holy smokes!" he exclaimed. "I'm about to be a dad!"

CRICKET WAS HUGE. She knew she looked quite unlike anything Jack might remember about her. It felt as if babies were popping out all over, taking up residence inside her thin frame, squeezing her out of shape from every side. This was not the way she wanted him to see her—but she had no choice. If they were to have any future together, she knew she couldn't keep him from the birth of his children.

She'd thought long and hard about when she felt safe enough to allow him back into her life. The time had never been right. She missed him, but she had also worried that nothing about their worlds could ever be right together. She'd procrastinated long enough that suddenly, she found herself on bed rest.

Then she hadn't wanted to call him, hadn't wanted him to see her in a vulnerable state. She grew like a snowball going downhill, picking up size and girth as it rolled, and her vanity wouldn't allow her to surrender her figure to his eyes.

Then, today, Dr. Suzanne said she could wait no longer. The babies were as big as they could be inside her small frame; everything was straining. She'd held them inside her as long as she possibly could.

Cricket had no choice but to call Jack and let him know he was about to be a father. He'd sounded so shocked—and delighted.

She folded the last of her things for the hospital, smiled at the three white bassinets lined up in the nursery and jumped when the doorbell rang. Her heart zipped nervously inside her—she recognized Jack's impatient call through the door.

"Cricket! It's Jack!"

Slowly, she opened the door. It was hard to meet his gaze. Shyness swept her. Time apart had made her memory of him sharper, and yet somehow seeing him again brought home hard how handsome, how magnetic he was in person.

"Wow," he said, his gaze dropping to her stomach. His eyes were wide. "I—you're beautiful, Cricket." He handed her a bouquet of pink roses he'd been holding, blooms down, by his side, an afterthought he'd completely forgotten about in the shock of seeing her.

"I'm huge," she said shyly, not meaning to sound apologetic, but that's how her words sounded.

"Yeah," he agreed. "How do you feel?"

"Just huge. Come on in." She led him inside, feeling fat, fat, fat. The thin figure he'd once admired had certainly disappeared under several pounds of babies, and yet she wouldn't change a thing.

"You sit down," he said. "I'll take care of everything. Should you even be walking around?"

"Jack, I sent Mother home for acting just like that. And she needed some rest. I want you here, but I don't want to be hovered over. All right?"

He seemed to hesitate. "I don't know if I can promise you not to hover. It just seems like you need to be resting. I almost feel bad, Cricket, for what I've done to you."

She couldn't help a smile. "Believe it or not, this is the most amazing thing that's ever happened to me. I couldn't be happier."

"You couldn't be more beautiful," he said, "unless you were sitting or lying down, at which point I could relax."

It was a large hint and she realized how nervous he was. "If I sit, will you not pace?"

"Was it that obvious?"

"You're like a tightly wound jack-in-the-box." She grimaced. "I didn't mean to make a play on your name. Sorry about that."

"It's pretty much true. Suddenly I feel as if I have springs attached to my muscles, making me jumpy." He sat, his gaze searching her face. "You seem calm, though."

"I am." Somehow she felt better just by his presence. Her mother had been such a huge help, but as the big day neared, Eileen had begun to get nervous, antsy. They'd started to get on each other's nerves, which Cricket hated, because she could tell her mother was trying so hard to be helpful. Finally realizing that she, too, was tight and feeling guilty about Jack, she sent her mother home. It had been the right thing to do. "I would have called you sooner," she said, "but there was so much I needed to do on my own."

"As long as I'm here for the big show," he said, "I'm content. Excited, even. Scared. Lots of emotions."

"There's some wine in the cabinet," Cricket said, but Jack shook his head.

"No, thanks. I intend to share every emotion with you."

"Jack," she said suddenly, "I should have called to tell you how sorry I was that Thad punched you."

"Forget about it. I already have."

She so much wanted him to give her family a second chance, and yet they had treated him rather dreadfully. Looking into Jack's warm gaze, Cricket wondered if they could ever start over on new ground. She really wanted that.

"Hey, I'm serious," he said. "It wasn't important."

"You never called," she said.

"I understood you were going through a lot."

"Yes, but my family should have been more courteous."

"Nah," he said. "You're their only little girl."

"Well, Thad wants to make it up to you."

He looked at her, his brows raising, a little suspicion in his gaze. "Yeah?"

She nodded. "He wants to take you up for a jump."

"Ah. And does he want to pack my parachute for me?"

She looked at him. "I don't blame you for feeling that way."

He sighed. "I'm sorry. I know your brother doesn't want to push me out of a high-flying plane with a malfunctioning parachute. He's honest enough to at least try to kill me in person."

"Jack!" She knew he was teasing, but she couldn't help feeling protective of her brother. "You don't know Thad. He's a sweetie, really. He was so sorry about punching you."

He shrugged. "I'll pass on the jump, if it's all the same. Unless Thad wants to do some bonding over bull riding," he said, perking up. "That'd be a great way for us to celebrate those brother-in-law bonds."

"Maybe we'll wait on the bonding," she said.

"That's probably a good idea for now," he replied. "I'm going to be very busy for the next few years. I don't suppose you'd allow me to touch your stomach?"

he asked, his voice wistful. "I'm awfully curious to meet my new children."

"Go ahead," she said, not having the heart to refuse him. But when his hands closed over her stomach, Cricket's heart jumped into her throat. These wonderfully large, masculine hands had gotten her into trouble in the first place…and she still remembered the magic they could play on her oh-too-willing body. Every time Jack touched her, she felt the sweet temptation run hotly through her veins, and Cricket knew she'd never be able to tell this call-of-the-wild cowboy no—except about becoming his wife, except about moving to Union Junction, except about ever getting into his bed again.

Chapter Sixteen

Jack tried not to wince when Cricket said, "I'll sleep on the recliner tonight."

He hadn't expected an invitation into her bed, but to have her distance herself from him by sleeping in a recliner sort of hurt his feelings. "You're safe," he said, his tone brisk. "I'll take the recliner."

She looked at him, a heartbreakingly sweet face that had only grown more beautiful to him since her pregnancy. "I always sleep on the recliner," she said softly, "even when my mother helps me. Anyway, there are five bedrooms in this house. There's plenty of places to sleep."

"Why do you sleep in the recliner?" he asked, glad that she wasn't trying to avoid contact with him.

"The babies are restless at night. There are three fighting for space, and so when they start doing their gymnastics, as I call it, it's challenging for my body if I'm lying down. It's also hard to get up."

She was quite a bit larger than he'd expected her to

be. He thought about how his father had warned him that if he didn't get Cricket to the altar before the babies were born, he might never get her there. "You look lovely," he said, his voice hoarse. He got all choked up just thinking about the fact that this wonderful woman was having his babies—how much luckier could a man get?

"You wouldn't think I was attractive if you saw me undressed," she told him matter-of-factly. "You should see the support system Mom and I rigged underneath this kimono so that I can stand up."

He looked at the flowing, shapeless dress she wore. "You look like you're ready for a luau or a garden party. I would never guess you're carrying three children in there if I didn't know better. Are you sure our babies are big enough to survive?"

"I worry about that, too," she said softly. "But the doctor thinks they each will weigh around five pounds. In my mother's generation, a five- to six-pound baby was considered healthy. I try not to scare myself to death over things I can't control."

"No, no," he said hastily. "And I don't know the first thing about pregnancies, anyway."

"Well, we'll know more tomorrow. I'm glad you're here," she said with a gentle smile at him.

He didn't know what to say to that. Why hadn't she called him sooner? Why hadn't she agreed to marry him?

It hit him that this woman had changed his life, changed him. And he had never seen it coming. Like a strong wind, she'd blown him over. "So you'll sleep out here," he said, "because it's more comfortable and not because you're worried about me—"

"I've slept in this recliner for the past month," Cricket told him.

"And you'll call me if you need anything in the night, even just getting up to use the, you know, go into the powder room," he said delicately.

She nodded. "I'm in your hands. Completely."

He took a deep breath. "I won't let you down."

She looked at him. "I know. That's why I called you. You're the one person I want by my side when I go through this."

He felt better knowing that she trusted him. "Good night," he said, and though he didn't kiss her good night, he wanted to more than anything.

"Jack?"

"Hmm?" He paused in the act of checking out the sofa. Could he sleep there? It didn't seem right to go sleep in a comfy room in the back while she was stuck in the recliner. Shouldn't he keep vigil with her tonight? What if she needed something suddenly and he didn't hear her?

"How's your mother?"

He looked at Cricket. "She's fine. Why do you ask?"

"I just wondered."

He looked in her eyes, sensing a deeper question. "You're asking if we're getting along."

She hesitated. "I suppose so."

"And you're wondering if I'm living at the ranch, getting along with Mom and making my father happy."

"I haven't heard much about you," she said, her gaze direct. "I do wonder if the black sheep is making its way back home."

"Mom's fitting in to Union Junction just fine."

She smiled. "You know I meant you, Jack."

"I never really considered myself a black sheep," he said, settling onto the sofa. "And I'd appreciate your not referring to me as such in front of the children. They can hear everything you say, you know." He slipped off his boots, arranged himself among the pretty flowered pillows, slid his hat down over his eyes.

"You're avoiding the question about your mother," she prompted.

"Not so much," he said, "but I'm still working on my million, if you're wondering about that."

"I see," she said, and he removed his hat to turn and stare at her.

"Why? Thinking about moving to the ranch?"

She shrugged. "I consider all our options."

"Hey," he said, "are you having second thoughts about being the wild girl of Fort Wylie?"

Her chin lifted. "Maybe, cowboy, maybe I am."

He sat up, his heart suddenly beating very quickly. "I don't suppose you'd be offering me any kind of proposal, would you?"

"Not marriage," she said hastily, "just...parenting together."

"Oh." He sank back into his reclining position. "Give a guy false hope, why don't you. Sheesh."

"I know it would be best for the children if we raised

them together, I just haven't figured out how we'd manage it."

"Glad you're slowly coming around to my side," he said, feeling grumpy.

"I'm just trying not to tie you down," Cricket said.

"You're the one avoiding the rope."

She sighed. "I know you have a lot of family things to attend to. I don't want to be a distraction."

"You *are* a distraction, whether you want to be or not. You're carrying my children. Where else do you think my mind is most of the time?" He sighed, wishing it were tomorrow already, wishing he knew whether his children would be born with all their tiny fingers and toes intact, whether they would be as pretty as their mother, wishing he knew something about being a father. "Listen, Pop's fine. He married Sara and they're the happiest couple you ever saw. She makes him lots of salads and other things she calls cleansing foods for his kidneys. Pop complains that all he wants in life is a cookie and maybe a double-fudge cake, and Sara smiles and gives him a different variation of something healthy and they're both happy. Mom seems to like living at the ranch. She gets lots of visits from grand-children, and this time I think she'll stay. She prefers the guesthouse, and I stay in the main house, but still, I come across her from time to time. She's gardening in a huge way and has been studying herbs. Says she's going to plant a bigger garden next year. Wants you to pick out drapes when you have time, maybe also next year," he said begrudgingly. "I swear that's what she said. But no pressure. We've survived without new drapes for many years, we may never get them." He felt pretty glum about that, just because he knew it was something his father had felt was important to the house. Actually, he knew his father only kept the ranch house because he had some mysterious connection to it, one that seemed to be growing even on Jack. "Weirdly, Pop claims there's ghosts in the house."

"What kind of ghosts?"

"Friendly ghosts. Misplaced ones who decided to take up residence there. They're from France," he explained. "It's not a reaction from the kidney surgery, as far as I can tell—he really believes there are ghosts there."

Cricket smiled. "Your father is awesome."

"No, really," Jack said, certain that Cricket thought he was just spinning a tale. "Pop swears they came from France to pull him through the surgery."

"Why aren't they living with him and Sara, then?"

"Because they need a grail. They're on a quest," he explained. "And Pop says they're in a snit because he left them in his templary, so they chose to follow him." He wondered how much he could share with her about the ghosts and decided to go all the way with this one. "Cricket, every once in a while, I could almost believe they're there, which I feel pretty weird saying to a deacon, because I'm pretty sure you don't believe in ghosts. Maybe angels, but not ghosts."

Cricket giggled. "I believe anything you tell me."

"You don't." He closed his eyes again. "If you did,

you'd believe that you and I need to get married for the sake of the children."

"Ugh," Cricket said. "Let's stay on the subject of ghosts. It's safer. How many are there?"

"Three," Jack said. "The house definitely feels fuller with them around."

"Eek," Cricket said. "I'm not staying at the ranch house anytime soon."

"Oh, a little ghost or three wouldn't chase you off," Jack said, feeling grumpy again. "You've got other reasons you won't come live with me."

"True," Cricket said. "I don't see myself anywhere but here."

He didn't, either. The old house with its quaint gingerbread trim suited her. There were baby presents along one wall, waiting to be opened, cards expressing well wishes for Cricket's pregnancy lined a sideboard. "I'd move here but I'm determined to outlast the old man's stubbornness. He thinks I can't stay in one place for more than a few moments. Mom says she thinks I should lighten Dad's wallet of a million dollars if for no other reason than to show him I can stick to one place. Be a family man."

"I agree with your mother," Cricket said. "Most people never see that much money. And a job is a job. Although I heard that the Lonely Hearts Station rodeo is coming up soon." She considered him for a moment. "I'm sure you miss your old life, Jack."

He turned to look at her again. "Who told you about the rodeo? Laura? Suzy? Priscilla?"

"They stopped by the other day," she said, her gaze innocent.

"And filled you in on things you shouldn't be troubling your pretty little head about," Jack said.

"Maybe not, but my pretty little head likes to know what the father of my two girls and one boy is doing."

He sat up. "Two girls and one boy?"

She nodded. "Yes, cowboy. I wasn't going to tell you, I was going to let you be surprised during the delivery, but I can't keep the news to myself any longer."

"Man," he said. "That's like hitting the lottery!" He jumped off the sofa, paced around the room for a moment. "Cricket, you *have* to marry me."

She shook her head. "'Have to' is something I opted out of when I gave up my church position."

He caught his breath. "Is that why you did it? Because you didn't want to feel forced to marry me?" He'd sensed that the women in the waiting room at Dr. Suzanne's hadn't felt anything but caring toward their deacon.

"Yes," she said. "I knew I wasn't going to get married, and I felt that they deserved a deacon who was living a bit more holy than I was."

His heart sank. "Still feel that way?"

She nodded. "To be honest, I've received a number of visits to reassure me that my position is waiting for me whenever I want it. But I know I'm doing the right thing."

Which meant she had no intention of ever marrying him. Jack realized he was walking in a supersize patch of trouble. "Why did you tell me all this after you mentioned the rodeo? Is there a connection?"

"Sort of," Cricket said. "It's my way of letting you know that I understand about rodeo. I know you understand about my love of parachuting. And that we'll have to figure out a way to be parents while understanding that we had a miracle of three babies, but we'll have to agree to be partners."

He frowned. "Partners? That sounds like new-age labeling for 'Cricket and Jack will be single parents'."

She didn't reply.

"Okay," he said, "I think I get it. You're telling me that you'll let me hang around and help you raise the babies from afar. I'll live in Union Junction and you'll live in Fort Wylie. You jump and I'll ride, and somehow in there, while we're living completely separate lives, we'll raise kids who somehow miraculously understand that Mommy and Daddy are too weird to be committed to each other." He paused. "Maybe the word I'm looking for is *selfish*. That's how it seems to me, anyway."

Cricket's brown eyes flashed at him. "Do you have a better suggestion?"

"No," he said, "because talking about this is going to make us both crazy. The obvious answer from a less involved person is that we should have used a condom or never gone to bed together, but frankly, Cricket, that would be like saying I don't want these children, and I darn well do. I also want you." He let out a deep breath and wondered why he wanted her right now, this minute, in the worst way. If nothing else, he'd like to be able to hold her, reassure her that everything was going to be all right, and "they" were going to be all right, but he couldn't hold her, she was ensconced in that recliner. All she needed was a moat around her and she'd be completely protected from him. Never had he known a woman with as much resistance as she gave him. "Let's get some sleep. Tomorrow's going to be a busy day, and the coaching tape I've been watching says the coach needs his rest the night before his children come into the world. Supposedly, birthing day is just like Christmas, only about a thousand times better."

He pushed his hat down low over his eyes. It hurt to know that his children wouldn't have a traditional family. Though his parents hadn't stayed together, they'd started out as a family and he remembered that it was later, when his mother had left, that his father had changed, turning into a sour, angry man.

It was important to have both parents around. He didn't like Cricket's plan, not one bit, but she was a stubborn girl, and he had lots of experience with stubborn. He had a father who was, and a mother who was, and brothers who knew something about stubborn and Templar knights living in his ranch house who'd stubbornly decided they were part and parcel of Josiah's legacy. Truly, Jack wasn't afraid of stubborn.

He'd just wait his deacon out. He would out-stubborn them all.

A father had to be strong. Now he understood Josiah, and loved him more for what he'd taught him about being a real father. Over the years, people—even Jack—had said that Josiah Morgan was a jackass. But now Jack knew that Josiah had simply been strong.

Chapter Seventeen

Cricket knew that she loved Jack. She always had. But right now, while she was being prepped for surgery, she wished she hadn't asked him to come.

She had never seen him nervous. She'd seen him hanging on to a wildly charging bull with a grin on his face. She'd seen him face down an angry father, a possible kidney operation, all with not a trace of fear or anxiety.

Right now, Jack Morgan was more nervous than she was. He was trying hard not to be; he was working hard at being a good coach, a soothing presence.

But she could feel how tense he was. He kept swallowing, his Adam's apple jerking uncomfortably. An active man, Jack never liked to be still, but the kindest description of what he was trying hard not to do was pace. The very fact that he was trying to stay in one place was unsettling—she would far rather he pace and let loose some of his nerves.

He gave her a weak smile and Cricket sighed. "It's going to be fine, Jack," she told him.

"Darn tootin' it's going to be fine," he said. "I've already given the doctor her pep talk."

"Pep talk?"

"Yes." He nodded adamantly. "She is not to hurt you. You are not to feel any pain. She's not to drop my children, nor traumatize them in any way. I want everything soft and comforting for everyone." He took a deep breath, passed a handkerchief over his brow. "This is hard work."

She smiled. "Why don't you go get a cup of coffee." She thought something more fortifying would be even better but didn't dare suggest that to him. Perhaps if he just left for a bit, the surgery would be over and he'd be a new father.

"No," Jack said. "The doctor says I'm doing fine."

Cricket smiled. "Dr. Suzanne has the patience of Job."

"Yes, well, she said that if I get any more nervous, she's going to have a pretty nurse give me a sedative in my riding cushions and I'll miss all the fun." He looked aggrieved. "I'm not nervous. I can't understand what she's referring to."

Cricket couldn't help her broad smile. "I like you like this."

"Like what?"

"With emotions." She looked at him. "You always seemed so coldhearted before."

"I was never coldhearted to you, Deacon."

"I don't know," she said softly. "I never felt like you could give your heart completely to anyone or anything.

Then I saw you trying to help Josiah, and I began to think there was more to you than just pride."

"I think I'm about to break a sweat, and all this talk of being coldhearted makes me want to show you just how hot I am for you."

"Oh," she said, "not with me wearing this silly hair covering and big as a house."

"Especially with you wearing that green hair covering and even bigger than a house."

"Jack!"

Dr. Suzanne laughed as she came to stand beside them. "I heard that, Mr. Morgan. You're supposed to re-assure my patient, not give her a complex."

"I can't give her a complex," Jack grumbled. "She had plenty of those before I came along. I'm just trying to work them out of her."

"Is that true, Cricket?" Dr. Suzanne asked with a smile.

"It's a strange form of seduction, Dr. Suzanne, but I suppose I had to choose a wild one to father my children."

"All right, Dad," Dr. Suzanne said, "stand to the side of Cricket, please. Let's find out if you're as good at birth coaching as you are at rodeo."

"Yeesh," Jack said, grabbing Cricket's hand, deter-mined to be supportive. "I heard you tell my father that I was only fair at rodeo."

"It was best he know the truth," Cricket said sweetly.

"I see how this relationship goes," Dr. Suzanne said. "You two are in the early 'in-love' phase. It's a fun time. My husband and I remember it fondly." She smiled as she teased them.

Jack raised a brow. "Early love? Cricket's never said she loved me. Do you know something I don't?"

Dr. Suzanne laughed. "Not me. I'm just the obstetrician. Okay, Cricket, are you ready for the biggest moment of your life?"

Cricket glanced at Jack for the quickest fraction of a second and thought, *He's the biggest moment of my life.*

Of course, she would never tell him that. She was pretty certain that the key to a heart as wild as Jack's was to always be free to ride off into the sunset, wherever the sun set next. What would he say if she said, *Yes, Jack, I'll marry you*?

He'd be happy at first—that was the nature of a competitor. After a while, the bonds of matrimony would begin to chafe. And then what? Would they end up like Gisella and Josiah, who were only now learning to be friends?

THE MOST WONDERFUL moment of Jack's life, absolutely awe-inspiring and scary as hell, was when Dr. Suzanne placed his firstborn child in his arms. It was a girl with a perfectly round head and sweet lips, crying like nobody's business, and he couldn't believe anything so tiny could contain such a set of lungs. "Hey," he told the baby, "simmer down now. I've got you, little thing."

A nurse standing near him chuckled. "Babies cry when they're born. We grade them on it."

"Oh," he told the baby. "I think you're passing with flying colors."

The nurse took the baby from him, though he wasn't ready to let go of his daughter. Another nurse placed a second baby in his arms, this one also a daughter. Her head wasn't quite so round, but she had a light dusting of hair and a softer cry. "This one's not yelling as much," he told the nurse. "Didn't you say you were grading them?"

"Yes," the nurse said. "All babies are assigned a number."

"Hey," he told the baby. "Don't be a B student. Give us a good wail."

"No," the nurse said, laughing. "She's fine. Just fine."

"Whew," Dr. Suzanne said. "Mr. Morgan, you have two healthy infants."

"Two?" His head reared up. "I'm supposed to have three healthy infants."

"And so you do." The last baby was handed to him a few moments later, a nice, barrel-chested son, who was louder than both his sisters. Jack grinned. "This one's an A student," he said, his heart full to bursting. "Cricket, all these children take after you."

"I doubt anyone has ever told the deacon she's loud," Dr. Suzanne said. She looked at Cricket. "You did fine. How are you feeling?"

"I feel excited. Happy. Tired," Cricket said. "But mostly, I feel like holding my children."

Jack watched as each baby was given to Cricket. He watched mother and children bond in that special way that mothers can with their babies, and he realized that good mothers just simply had that connection. His heart full of understanding now for the pain that Gisella must have felt during her long years away, he resolved to be more understanding of his mother.

"Cricket," he said, going to her side, "you really are the most beautiful woman I've ever known. It's just in you, all the beauty a man looks for in a woman."

"Why, Jack," Cricket said, "whatever has gotten into you?"

He looked at his children squalling red-faced and adorable around their mother. "You," he said, "I think it's you."

"Are there names for the children?" a nurse asked.

Jack looked at Cricket. "Are there names for the children?"

Cricket said, "We haven't discussed names yet, but I have suggestions."

"Good," Jack said, "because they're not leaving this room as Baby Morgan A, B and C."

Cricket hesitated, frowned at Jack. He sensed he'd stepped in trouble again. "What?"

"Jasper," she said.

He blinked. "Jasper?"

"That's my last name."

He got it. "Oh, no," he said. "No, see, I'm a traditional guy. We may not be married, but we will be. And those children will bear the name of their father from day one. They're not going to be asked embarrassing questions on the playground like, *Where's your father?* and *Who's your daddy?* and *Why didn't your father love your mother enough to marry her?* No!" he said loudly, shaking his head. "Deacon, here's where I draw the line with my size-eleven boot. I've been asking for months. You're the one who's stubborn as a mule, but you're not going to saddle our babies with a lifetime of laughter and finger-pointing. Trust me, I know all about the questions kids ask other kids, and I'm very sensitive to this. You can pick the first names and the middle names—hell, pick all the names you want, but I've picked the last name and these children are all Morgans. Write it on the charts, Nurse. M-O-R-G-A-N, just like the horses."

Everyone, including Dr. Suzanne, stopped to stare at Jack. Cricket studied him for a long moment, then sighed. "All right," she said. "Gisella Eileen, Jonathan Josiah and Katie Rose."

"Morgan," Jack said.

"Morgan," Cricket echoed.

"Where does the Katie Rose come in?" Jack asked.

"My name is Katherine. Cricket is a nickname."

"I never knew that." Jack looked at her. "I like Katie. What about Rose?"

"I just like it," she said, lifting her chin.

"I don't know if I want my son named after me," Jack said. "And Pop's already got one namesake, thanks to Pete and Priscilla."

"If we're going traditional, let's do it all the way," Cricket said.

"The kids will call him JJ," Jack said.

"They didn't call you that."

He looked at her. "No, I've always been Jack."

Cricket closed her eyes, looking tired for the first time. Dr. Suzanne finished examining her stitches and said, "Now that we've got that solved, let's let everyone get some rest."

"That sounds good to me," Jack said, "Cricket, can I get you something?"

"Yes," she said, sounding sleepy, "a wedding ring."

Jack glanced at Dr. Suzanne. "Did she say what I thought she said?"

A nurse checked Cricket's pulse. Dr. Suzanne stepped close to the bed. The babies were taken away, wheeled down to the nursery in their plastic bassinets. Jack had been relieved that they hadn't seemed to require any type of serious extra care.

"Cricket," Dr. Suzanne said, "did you say you needed something?"

Cricket opened her eyes for a second. "I think sleep will do me just fine, Doctor, thank you."

Dr. Suzanne shrugged at Jack. "We'll take her to her room now."

Jack nodded, let down like all get out.

"Congratulations, Mr. Morgan," Dr. Suzanne said. "Three healthy babies is a lot to be thankful for."

"Yes," he said, wishing that Cricket really did want the one thing he didn't seem to be able to give her.

Chapter Eighteen

When Cricket awakened, Jack wasn't in the hospital room like she thought he'd be. The nurse saw her anxious look.

"Dad's down at the nursery," she said with a smile, and Cricket relaxed. She couldn't explain it, but his face was the one she'd wanted to see when she woke up. She wanted to see her babies, too, but she had an overwhelming need to see Jack.

It was almost as if she was afraid that he might leave and not come back to see her. She knew he would always want to see his children. He talked a lot about wanting to marry her and she'd always pushed that suggestion away, fearing that he'd tire of her once his wanderlust took over again—and then something had told her that she was the one doing the damage by being nervous about the same thing his father had been nervous about. There was no reason to put distance between herself and Jack because of rodeo. Rodeo was the symbol of a way of life Jack loved—he'd never said he planned to give it up, and he'd never said he loved her. Not in so many words, but he had offered her a commitment. And one thing she'd realized someplace between the amazing birth of her children and the joy that they had all come through the experience just fine was that Morgan men stayed committed to their women. Even now, though years had passed between Josiah and Gisella's marriage, Josiah was still committed to Gisella's well-being.

She had nothing to fear from Jack. No matter what happened between them, he was never going to ride off into the sunset and forget about her.

Perhaps she'd worried knowing about the animosity between father and son. But that had been smoothed over, perhaps even more than just a leveling of old anger. Sometimes she thought she sensed genuine affection growing between the two. Even with his mother, Jack seemed to be making an effort to reestablish their relationship, something that had to be hard after so many years apart.

He didn't even seem that concerned that her brother had taken a shot at him. She was more angry with Thad than Jack. Jack had shrugged it off. Her parents had given him a rather reserved welcome, and Jack hadn't opposed her naming one of the children after her mother.

Contrary to everything she'd ever known or heard about Jack, he didn't seem to hold a grudge past the point of necessity. Affection and responsibility for his family appeared to come more easily to him than anyone—and maybe even Jack—had ever thought it would.

Time would tell.

Of course, she didn't have much time. She hadn't told Jack this yet, but her parents and Thad had offered to take over her tea shop and run it themselves. They had a hankering for a family business, and a sweet tooth that wanted to see the tea shop stay operating. With three newborns in Cricket's life, they worried she wouldn't have the time or energy to run the shop. This solution would keep her business in the family, and it would allow her to move to Union Junction, which, as they pointed out, she might have to do at some point for the sake of the children. Cricket would even make money monthly, as her family intended to divide the business in quarters. It was a sound idea, and it left Cricket with no financial reason to stay in Fort Wylie.

But she knew she couldn't pack up and follow a certain rodeo man without a plan, either.

JACK KNEW the cavalry had arrived by the sound of many voices raised with anxious delight. Voices that he recognized, knew and loved well, made his heart expand. His family was on the premises, heading straight for the nursery. A large group of people rounded the corner, every member accounted for except Josiah.

"Jack!" Laura, Priscilla and Suzy exclaimed, rushing to hug him.

"Show us our new family members," Laura told him, and with the proudest grin he'd ever worn, Jack pointed through the glass.

"Ah," Gisella said, "two girls and a boy!"

"One named after you, Gisella," Sara said. "If Josiah could see them, he'd be so proud." She began taking pictures on her camera phone, despite the glass. "Josiah's on pins and needles to see pictures," she told Jack. "It was all I could do to make him stay home and rest."

"How's Pop doing?"

Sara and Gisella smiled. "He's antsy," Sara said. "But when the children come to visit, he's much better."

Pete, Gabe and Dane came to shake his hand. "Good going," Dane said as Pete helped lift some of the Morgan brood to the window to see their new cousins.

"Thanks," Jack said. "But I didn't do any of the work."

Gabe laughed. "You did *something*."

"Three babies," Gabe said. "Who would have ever thought Jack Morgan would be a father to three?"

"Not me," Jack said. "I'm still in shock."

"But they're the most beautiful babies you ever saw, right?" Pete asked.

Jack grinned. "How did you know?"

"I just did," Pete said. "How's Cricket? And when are you going to get her to Union Junction?"

"That I don't know," Jack said. "Maybe never. But she was amazing. She made the whole thing look easy." Jack was pretty sure he could never carry children and then birth them—it was pretty good being the dad and watching everything from a few feet away. "The doctor says Cricket can go home in a few days."

"Home to Fort Wylie?" Gabe asked, and Jack nodded. "I think that's going to be our home."

"Well," Pete said. "It'll only cost you a million dollars. Pop will say you were always the black sheep or some nonsense. He did mutter that you were the only one of his children who had his babies born outside of Union Junction."

Jack scratched his head as he listened to the women coo over the babies. He stared through the window at his progeny, loving the sight of tiny fingers and faces. He'd never planned this moment in his life; never thought he'd have kids. "Baby steps," he murmured. "Tell Pop to relax. I'm just taking baby steps."

Pete clapped him on the back. "That's right. Just enjoy the moment. Being a dad is the best."

Jack nodded, agreeing. But being a dad and a husband would be better. He intended not to let Josiah's warning about never getting a woman to the altar after the babies were born come true.

"Hello!" Jack heard, turning to see Thad and Cricket's parents arriving for their first peek at the babies.

"Aren't they beautiful—" Eileen exclaimed, giving Jack a brief hug. Reed shook his hand more awkwardly, and Thad hung back just a split second before offering his hand as well. Jack performed the niceties, introducing Cricket's parents to his huge family, and then some strained silence ensued.

Then Gisella said, "These babies are so lucky to have so many people who want to hold them!" and that seemed to melt the ice a little. Although Jack wondered if it would have thawed at all if Josiah had been there.

Josiah wasn't going to think much about Cricket

and Jack living in Fort Wylie, and Jack began to wonder if he could spend much time with these frosty in-laws who clearly wondered what their daughter saw in him.

THE NEXT FEW DAYS were spent learning how to bathe the babies, breast-feed the babies and letting Cricket get her strength back. Cricket seemed to take to mothering like a bird to the air, and Jack felt his role was pretty much being a support system.

In fact, he was beginning to feel oddly as if he wasn't of much importance to the parenthood equation. He fetched tasty snacks to tempt Cricket and he held babies, but mostly he was beginning to feel like the human equation of the car hood ornament—just there for show.

Flowers arrived in a steady stream for Cricket and Jack—many from his rodeo friends. His cell phone buzzed with texts keeping him up-to-date on circuit happenings—and on the morning of their last day in the hospital, Jack received a text that caught his interest.

The committee has obtained a new sponsorship. This year's top rodeo prize in Lonely Hearts Station will be worth a million dollars!

Jack's jaw dropped. That was a lot of dough.

He'd won at the last rodeo in Lonely Hearts Station.

A *million*-dollar purse. The same amount Pop was offering for something Jack wasn't sure he could give. But rodeo was what Jack did best. Bull riding was a piece of cake compared to living with family angst.

"Jack?" Cricket said. "You look like you're deep in thought."

The babies had been wheeled to the nursery for baths after their feeding. Cricket gazed at him, her pretty eyes sleepy now. She wasn't taking a lot of pain medication, but Dr. Suzanne had warned him that Cricket needed lots of rest.

And he needed to think. "You go to sleep," Jack told her. "I'm going to head out for a bit. I'll shower at your house, and you get some sleep."

"All right." She smiled at him, then closed her eyes.

He looked at Cricket for a long moment before he left, his mind racing.

Chapter Nineteen

"What do you mean, Jack's entered the Lonely Hearts Station rodeo?" Josiah demanded, staring at his three sons who'd come to visit him. He felt fine, he was tired of everybody coddling him, and he could tell by the expression on Gabe's, Dane's and Pete's faces that they'd debated the wisdom of telling him. *They didn't want to upset me*, Josiah thought to himself, annoyed that everybody seemed to think he needed protection from the bumps and bruises of life. "Tell me everything and quit holding out on me."

Pete sighed. "He entered. He rides tomorrow."

Josiah's eyes bugged. "He didn't tell you, did he?"

"No." Gabe shook his head. "We found out about it completely by accident. I saw Mimi and Mason Jefferson in town and they mentioned it." He shrugged. "My best guess is that Jack doesn't want us to know. Doesn't feel he needs a cheering section."

"Hell's bells," Josiah said. "You can bet Cricket doesn't know, either. She would have mentioned it to Priscilla, at least."

Dane nodded. "That's a pretty safe assumption."

"So why's he doing it? The rascal!" Josiah shook his head. "His babies are only two weeks old! He needs to stay home with Cricket and the children. He can't spend his life on the road anymore." Josiah's white brows quivered above suddenly bright eyes. "There better be a durn good reason."

"A million dollars," Pete said, and Josiah blinked.

"All he has to do for that is live at the ranch for a year. Same deal you boys got."

"Yeah," Gabe said, "but Jack's always done things his way."

Josiah sniffed. "He should be at home helping Cricket, not running after a fool's dream that may only net him some broken bones."

Dane shrugged. "Don't think he wants our opinions or he would have told us and we wouldn't have heard about it through the grapevine."

"True," Josiah said, reaching for one of Pete's small babies when it started to cry. He held the child against his chest, looked at Sara. "I'm sure you have a pearl of wisdom to toss out here."

"No," Sara said, lifting the crust on a cherry pie. "This is done to a turn. Who wants a piece?"

"I do," the four men said, and Sara laughed.

"Good." She started to cut the pie, noticed the frown on Josiah's face. "Whipped cream on top?" she asked.

"I trust you for your honesty," Josiah said, and Sara sighed.

"Once upon a time you asked me what you should

do if Jack were to give you his kidney and then still want to ride rodeo. I said that you should go watch him. After all, you'd be well, and this is Jack being Jack. Why waste time keeping distance?" She handed out plates to appreciative men. "Life is short. I say we all go, and we all applaud, no matter the outcome."

"What if Cricket doesn't know?" Josiah asked gruffly. "Won't it seem as if we withheld information from her?"

"That's not my affair," Sara said. "Nor is it yours. All we can do is support Jack in his efforts. For all you know, he wants to win that million dollars so he can tell you he's moving to Fort Wylie."

"That's what I'm afraid of! He just wants to tell me to shove off!" Josiah exclaimed, and Sara dropped a kiss on his forehead.

"I know, you old fussbudget," she said fondly. "This time, you're going to have to tough it out. You can't control your kids anymore—this one may earn his way right out of your control and into Cricket's world."

"I'll pick out my clothes for tomorrow," Josiah said. "let's at least caravan out there and show that the Morgans are backing one of their own. I swear, I may need a new ticker if Jack gets stomped."

"You'll need a new ticker if you keep eating this pie," Pete said appreciatively. "Sara, you should enter this pie in the state fair."

Josiah sighed to himself and kept his fretting silent. All the money in the world couldn't tame Jack. His eldest son was going to do things *his* way—he always had—and this time, Josiah was going to show him how proud he was.

CRICKET WAS WORRIED about Jack. She knew enough about her man to know that he was quiet. Too quiet. It wasn't just that he was tired from helping her with the babies. He was a huge help—even her mother had commented on how devoted Jack was to making sure she and the babies had everything they needed. Her heart had been warmed by her mother's slow-won approval.

She wondered if he regretted making love to her, then knew she was being silly, suffering some type of postpartum blues. Jack had never once complained. In fact, he seemed to adore the babies. One day she'd gotten up, surprised by how rested she felt and walked out to the den to find all three infants sleeping on a nice soft pallet, their father asleep not two feet away on the sofa.

Now that she was formula-feeding—she hadn't had much luck with breast-feeding, though Jack had been endlessly encouraging—he'd taken over the making of the bottles with relentless precision. He made notes about each baby's feeding in a notebook. And diapering, he said, was no different than roping—you just had to be fast while the little buggers did their best to get away.

That had made her laugh.

But for the past two days, Jack had been so preoccupied that she was beginning to get nervous. Probably he needed a break from the schedule of three newborns. "No doubt Jack must feel housebound," she confided to Thad when he came over to visit one afternoon.

"Absolutely," Thad said. "I'd be going stir-crazy."

"I know I am," Cricket said, and Thad looked at her.

"Take a jump," he suggested.

"I would love to," she murmured, knowing full well what Jack's response to that would be.

"A couples jump is good for closeness," Thad said, and Cricket's heart leaped inside her.

It would be wonderful. That's exactly what they needed. But Jack would never agree. "I don't think he'd go for it."

"Maybe not right away," Thad said. "It may take a little more time to get used to the idea. He'll come around."

"Maybe," she said, not sure about that.

"I'm a little surprised you're not at the rodeo," Thad said. "I actually came over to see if you needed a babysitter."

She looked at Thad. "Babysitter? You?"

He shrugged. "You don't think I can take care of my nieces and nephew?"

"Well, I—what rodeo?"

"The Lonely Hearts Station rodeo."

She shook her head. "Why would I?"

"You went last year," Thad pointed out. "And the father of your children is a bull rider, right? I just thought it made sense that you would."

"Oh." Cricket slowly got up to rearrange some toys. Some days her stitches still hurt. Her body didn't feel quite itself just yet, but she was secretly delighted with her progress. She'd lost a healthy amount of weight and felt good. Jack had helped with that. Every once in a while, when he thought she didn't know he was doing it, she'd catch him checking out her legs or her breasts. In general, he seemed to keep his gaze on her often, which made her feel attractive. "Jack hadn't mentioned he wanted to go this year."

Thad didn't reply. Cricket had assumed Jack had gone to visit his father today—when he'd left the house, he'd merely said he'd be back later tonight. She glanced over at her brother, hesitating as she saw him watching her, his face concerned. "What?"

"Nothing," he said quickly.

"*Something,*" she said, an old routine between them. "Something's on your mind."

"Not so much. Just these little babies," he said, getting down on the floor to watch them as they lay on the thick pallet Jack had fixed for them.

Cricket liked the pallet better than the bassinet because the babies seemed to like lying together, cuddled up next to each other. They looked like peas in a pod, and she had taken tons of pictures of them. *Angels,* she thought. *These babies are angels. Funny how Josiah thought he had ghosts at the ranch house.* And then it hit her.

"Jack's riding today, isn't he?" she demanded.

Thad cleared his throat.

"Thad!" she exclaimed, sensing her brother's reluctance to be the bearer of bad news.

"Oh, come on," he said. "Don't make me be the rat fink."

She was going to kill both the men in her life, her brother because he was being a wienie, and Jack for not telling her about his plans. Of course, she wasn't his wife, he could do as he pleased, but… "I don't understand why he didn't tell me."

"Fear of failure." Thad shook a rattle for the babies, who seemed more interested in their toes. "Fear of disappointing you? I don't know."

"Why are men so complex?" Cricket demanded. *Particularly mine?*

"Fears," Thad said. "Men have a lot of them."

"Oh, baloney. I spent years counseling couples and I never—" Cricket paused, thinking about all the couples she'd talked to, learning their private stories. Usually, couples felt that their partner wasn't listening to them, and that lay at the root of their problems. It was all about miscommunication, and clearly she and Jack were also misfiring on that front. "I changed for him," she said, "he didn't change for me."

Thad blinked. "That doesn't sound right, but I can't quite put my finger on the improper logic."

"Probably not." Cricket took a deep breath. "But he just can't decide he's going to slip off without telling me."

"Wait," Thad said. "Rodeo is how the man makes a living, isn't it? Do you think he just went to work, like any other man would? Jack probably didn't think it was earth-shattering news that he was going to try to make a buck."

"Why are you taking his side?" Cricket asked.

"I'm not. I'm trying to dig my way out of trouble. I

don't like to cause trouble," Thad said, "and I don't want Jack to think I'm a weasel for telling on him."

"I gave up jumping because of him," Cricket said, starting to steam, "and he had no intention of giving up rodeo!"

"Wait," Thad said, holding up the rattle. "You didn't give up parachuting because of the cowboy. You were pregnant, Cricket! Be reasonable."

She was trying to be. But she was hurt Jack wouldn't confide in her. She'd been worrying about him feeling tied down when obviously he was just going on with his life, while she…she had decided to give up an activity she loved, knowing he didn't want her doing it.

"Have you guys talked about this giving-up thing?" Thad asked.

Cricket shook her head.

"Well, I wouldn't get myself in a knot, then."

Cricket knew her brother was right. "I'll take you up on that babysitting offer."

He looked at her. "I'm happy to do it, but do you think this is wise? Are you cleared to drive yet? Maybe you should just talk to him when he gets home."

"I want to see Jack ride," Cricket said.

"For support?"

She wasn't sure. But this was who Jack was, and Cricket knew that. Rodeo was so much a part of him that even Josiah hadn't been able to threaten, bluster or buy it out of Jack's life. "Not just support," Cricket said, "but because I'm not going to live the next fifty years of my life with a man who's afraid to tell me what he loves in life."

"Okay," Thad said, "that sounds healthy."

She intended for their relationship to be very healthy. "And schedule a jump for me," Cricket said, "one month from today."

"Shouldn't you talk to Jack first?"

Cricket headed to her room to change. "You just worry about being Uncle Thad today and put away your counselor's hat." The truth was, she wasn't sure what to tell Jack. All she knew was that this rodeo was a defining moment in their relationship. She planned to make certain she and Jack didn't repeat history, drifting apart like Gisella and Josiah had when their marriage was young. She and Jack weren't even married, and that put them on shakier ground even than Gisella and Josiah's relationship had been.

She kissed each baby on the head and went out the door, anxious to catch Jack before he rode. Who knew what could happen?

Chapter Twenty

Cricket remembered the first time she'd ever seen Jack on the back of a thrashing bull—she remembered because that's when she'd fallen in love with him. It had been love at first sight. She'd known it; there'd been no escaping her unruly heart's longings for the cowboy.

This time was no different. She got to the rodeo just in time to see Jack's first ride, her breath nearly stopping in her chest as she watched him stick to the back of the bull the best he could. Arm held up high above his head trying for more points, Jack made it to the buzzer before being thrown to the ground.

She gasped, and knew better than to dash to the rail to check on him. In fact, she didn't want him to know she was there at all.

There was no point in making him nervous or unhappy, taking his mind off of his ride. She wanted him to do whatever it was he had set out to do.

She seated herself high up in the stands, away from where anyone she knew might see her. Jack's scores were announced and she proudly noted he had earned a respectable score. Surely he'd be pleased with that.

But she knew he wouldn't be completely pleased unless he won.

"Got a sweetie riding?" a nearby middle-aged woman asked her. She threw some peanut shells down and smiled warmly at Cricket.

"Um, just a friend," Cricket said. "You?"

"A son." The woman's smile turned a little rueful. "You know how it goes. Rodeo gets into their blood at a young age."

Cricket swallowed, thinking about her own baby boy. In six years or less, he'd be old enough for snatching the bow off the calf's tail games. Jack would probably want to buy him a tiny pony to practice riding on—of course he would. One step always led to another—

"I don't think he's got a shot at the million," her seatmate said. "There's too many cowboys in there with a lot more experience. Still, I'm hoping he does all right."

Cricket's blood went cold. "I'm sorry. What do you mean, a million?"

Her new friend's penciled brows nearly reached her hairline. She tossed down a few more peanut shells, munching happily. "The million-dollar purse," she said. "Guess anybody could use that much good luck, huh?"

Cricket's breath caught. Now she knew exactly why Jack was riding. It wasn't because he couldn't be tamed. She had said she wouldn't move to the Morgan ranch.

Jack had always said he wanted to be with her and the children. He fully intended to stay forever at her tea-shop home. A million dollars would replace the money he would give up by not fulfilling his father's wishes. And contrary to what she'd told his father when he was in the hospital, Jack had ridden very well at the last rodeo here. He had to figure his chances were just as good as the next cowboy's. Sudden anxious nerves assailed her. There was probably nothing worse to start out a relationship on than making someone feel that they had to change everything in their life because of you. Thad was right—Jack had made lots of changes for her. And lots of sacrifices. "Yes," she murmured, "anyone could use that much good luck."

She stood, giving the woman a smile. "Best of luck to you."

"You're not staying?"

Cricket shook her head. "I saw what I came to see."

She left, slipping out so that no one would be the wiser to her presence. She got into her vintage VW and drove home, saying a silent prayer that Jack's every ride would be safe and long.

But mostly safe.

JACK WAS HAPPY with his first ride, but the key was making all his rides good ones. He'd felt a strange pop in his knee as he'd landed on the ground and could tell his knee was aggravated, enough to swell a bit. When the round of rides finished, he checked the scores, seeing that he was in third place going into the next round tomorrow. Good enough. He had a chance. A million dollars was enough money to keep him in the game. He thought about Cricket and his tiny, fairly bald, sweeter-than-he-thought-they'd-be children, and knew he had to ride on.

He went to secretly ice his knee.

"THAT WAS PRETTY GOOD," Josiah said reluctantly. "But I still wish he'd just live at the ranch, Gisella."

Gisella and Sara smiled at him. Josiah shrugged. "Okay, I'm proud. He's a little bit better of a rider than I expected him to be."

Pete, Dane and Gabe looked at each other. Laura, Priscilla and Suzy had stayed home to watch the children, deciding to make a barbecue celebration for everyone when they returned.

"I thought he got up a bit slow," Pete commented.

"I did, too," Dane agreed.

"I thought Jack was just staying low, trying to see which way the bull was going to go," Gabe said, waving at his brothers to be quiet around Josiah.

Josiah turned his head to stare at his sons seated behind him. "What are you boys talking about?"

"Nothing, Pop," Pete said.

"I didn't see anything slow," Josiah said, "except maybe that clown."

"Yeah," Gabe said. "It's fine, Pop. No worries."

Josiah sniffed and turned back around. "You boys would know better than me what Jack normally looks like on a ride. But I thought he looked good."

"Had a new sponsor, too," Pete said.

"Probably got that because he's the rider with the most children," Gabe said, and they laughed.

"That's not funny," Josiah said. "You boys are too hard on your brother."

"We're just picking at you, Pop," Dane told him. "We can see your hair turning whiter by the second."

Josiah sighed. "You see how they treat me, ladies. I suffer."

Sara patted his arm. Gisella handed him some popcorn. They watched the next round begin and Josiah wondered how much stress one father could take. He, too, had seen Jack get up slow, and he was nervous. In fact, it was his worst nightmare. Jack wouldn't turn in his number over a little bump or bruise—or much else, either. Not with him sitting within a shot of the big prize. Josiah held in a groan and tried to focus on the fact that he was supposed to be having a great time sitting around with his family, watching Jack do what he loved, something he'd never been able to do before. He was a father, and sometimes, being a father was a really tough job. "Well, show's over for us for today," he said. "Let's head home and eat some barbecue. Tomorrow's a big day, and I want to be back bright and early."

CRICKET HAD JUST PUT the triplets down for their three-hour nighttime nap—they weren't sleeping through the night, nowhere close, of course—when Jack walked in. Limped in, she realized.

She didn't ask him about his injury. If he wanted to talk about it, he would.

"Hey," he said to her.

"Hi to you, too."

"How are the babies?"

She smiled. "They had a big day. They were a little hard to get down, but they're sleeping now."

He limped over to the sofa. She bit her lip, wanting desperately to ask him, knowing he wasn't about to share. He was so much like Josiah, after all.

"Can I help you get your boots off?"

He shook his head. "I got it. Thanks."

She watched him struggle with his boots, then turned away. Tea was what she did best, she decided, tea and prayer. "I was just about to make a nice soothing cup of tea. Can I get you one? And maybe some chocolate cookies? I like chocolate cookies when I'm not...I mean, at night."

He glanced at her. "Cricket, you don't have to wait on me. I'm living here to help you with the children. So how about you sit down, and I'll make the tea and cookies?" Getting up, he took her hand, gently guiding her toward the place where he'd been seated. "Tea and chocolate. I can handle that."

She closed her eyes as she sat, listening to him rifle through the kitchen. He was stubborn—had she ever realized how much?—and the best thing she could do was let him be himself. It hurt; she desperately wanted to take care of him. But by opposing his livelihood, she had put a distance between them that only time would breach. Casting about for a safe subject, she finally said, "I got an offer from a church today. It was on my message machine when I got home."

He set tea and cookies in front of her, like an offering from a prince. "Congratulations. I'd like to hear all about that after you tell me where you went today."

She'd slipped. Jack's eyes were on her, intent and interested. She could fib, but she wasn't going to. He would find out soon enough. "I went to watch you ride."

The tea cooled between them, the cookies sat untouched. Cricket had no appetite.

"I should have told you," Jack finally said, leaning into the seat across from her. "And may I just make the observation that you're not supposed to be driving yet."

"We should tell each other a lot of things," Cricket said. "Later on. When we have time. Right now, why don't you let me cut those jeans off of you and see what we can do about your knee."

He sighed. "I would actually appreciate that."

She carefully cut off his jeans, iced his knee with a bag of frozen peas and elevated it, grateful when he fell asleep on the sofa.

He looked exhausted. *This is what I signed on for when I fell for Jack Morgan,* she thought, gazing at him, dark and tired and incredibly handsome on her flowered sofa. *Thank God he came home to me and the children tonight.*

This was the starting point for everything to come, she decided. If Jack was going to be a road warrior, then she wanted him to know that he was always welcome to come back home to her.

Having him in her life was worth the agony of separation, worry, loneliness. Yes, Jack Morgan was worth it.

Chapter Twenty-One

Early the next morning, Thad, Eileen and Reed came over to watch the babies while Cricket drove a protesting Jack to Lonely Hearts Station.

"You're not supposed to be driving," Jack insisted.

To that, Cricket just said, "Hush."

"At least drive my truck. I know you're killing yourself driving that ancient Bug-thing." If he won the rodeo, Jack determined right then and there that he was buying Cricket a minivan. Something like a tank, with all-around air bags. The babies were due to visit the doctor any day now for their first checkup, and little Miss Independent would probably insist on driving herself. If his woman and his babies were going to be on the road constantly, especially if she accepted whatever job she'd been offered, then they were going to be as safe as he could make them. He filed her job offer under the Next Emergencies to Deal With in his brain, took a brief moment to consider whether he wanted a working wife, decided that if he interjected an opinion on that at this moment he'd probably get his head handed to him. Cricket had already taken his rodeoing without protest; he'd best keep his mouth shut while he was ahead.

Besides, until he got her to the altar, he had very little to zero say in her decisions, anyway. "My truck is newer," he said, fighting one small battle at a time. And Cricket finally said, "All right. You just lie back there and visualize winning."

He honestly didn't need to lie down; the swelling was almost gone. The knee felt a bit stiff but it wasn't enough to keep him from riding. "Why do I have the feeling that you're being very understanding, even for a deacon?"

"I have no idea," Cricket said, backing out of the driveway.

He gazed at the tea-shop side of the house as she drove away. It was quaint; he knew she loved it. But there was little yard for kids to play in and no place to keep ponies. Teaching the kids to ride was still a few years away; still, he dreamed about riding with his children. He thought about serving tea and cookies in their family tea shop, considered the fact that Cricket's parents had offered to buy the place and run it. She hadn't said anything lately about their offer; there was too much happening in her life for her to move now. Maybe if he won the million-dollar purse, he'd start a business, keep his wife at home.

She'd never said a word about the prize money, just offered silent support. "You're planning a jump, aren't you?"

Her eyes met his in the rearview mirror. "I did mention it to Thad. It's too soon right now, obviously, but it's been a long time. I'm ready to get back to my life."

Just like he was getting back to his were the unspoken words. "My dangerous love earns a living," he pointed out.

She said, "Let's have this debate later."

"Nah," he said. "Just go ahead and tell Thad that if the mother of my children jumps out of a plane, I'll return the punch he welcomed me to the family with."

They spent the rest of the trip to Lonely Hearts Station in silence.

JACK MORGAN WAS A PAIN in the patoot, Cricket thought, censoring her thoughts. Bossy, domineering… domineering…bossy. She grit her teeth, not about to fuss with him before he rode. With her luck, her stubborn cowboy would break his neck and the last words he would have heard from her would be *Punching my brother would be a mistake on your part, you bigheaded creep.* Cricket sighed. She loved Jack, even when he was annoying. Maybe attitude was part of his game-day preparation. She'd smooth that out of him later.

She parked outside the arena and he got out. There was no reason to say anything; she didn't know what he needed to hear before he rode, anyway. Did one say *Good luck* or *Break a leg?* Was he superstitious? She didn't know.

She squealed when he jerked the driver's-side door

open, shocked when he melted her with a steamy, heart-stealing kiss. His eyes blazed down at her when he finished, and then he walked away.

"Okay," she said after she'd recovered, "I think that was how we say good luck in Jack Morgan's world."

She liked it. Her heart was racing, she was nervous as all get out, but she wasn't about to not witness her man's two rides today, win, lose or fall.

JOSIAH HAD NEVER BEEN as anxious as he was today. "There's nothing worse than watching your son deliberately try to kill himself," he said, carping to everyone in the double-cab truck.

"Pop, it's going to be fine," Pete said, who was driving the brothers and Pop to Lonely Hearts Station. "Jack's been doing this for years."

"And as I recall, getting stomped a few times, too. I seem to remember a few—"

"Pop," Dane said, "don't get agitated. There's nothing you can do about it."

"There never was," Josiah said on a sigh.

"That's right," Sara said. "Now, just be proud."

"And be glad only one of our sons did this," Gisella said. "I don't think you could have survived the agony of more of them riding."

"Actually," Josiah said, reflecting back over the years, "want to know what scared me the worst?"

"Not really," Gabe said, and everybody laughed.

"What scared me the most was my other three sons going into the military. Now *that* made for some sleepless nights." Josiah looked out the window, watched the landscape rush by. He'd been proud of their service to country, durn proud, knew they needed to do it. But he'd spent a lot of worried nights around the world, wondering if he'd stayed home more, if his boys would have known him better, wanted to be with him.

"You never said that before," Dane said.

Josiah snorted. "What do you think? I had a Texas Ranger, a spy, a soldier and a bull rider for sons. Did you think I had a heart made of iron?"

"Yes!" everybody in the truck exclaimed at once, then laughed. Josiah knew they were teasing him, but they were wrong. It was a wonder he hadn't needed a new heart instead of a kidney.

"Well, I did," he said, okay with playing Tough Pop for the occasion. "I had to be strong to survive the lot of you."

"We know, we know," Gabe said, chuckling, but Josiah didn't care that they were teasing him. Almost all of his boys had come home—he figured he'd gotten everything he wanted, and then some.

CRICKET PUT HER HANDS over her eyes when the bull charged from the gate, accompanied by the announcer yelling, "Mighty Jack Morgan, riding Hell-Beast! Come on, come on, Morgan!" She peeked through her fingers, her heart completely arrested in her chest. Up and down Jack went, mimicking the rolling, thrashing motions of the bull. Never had time passed so slowly. Never had she been so afraid. This was nothing like jumping out of a plane; watching your man at the mercy of a bull with nothing but his wits was horrible. She was so proud, she didn't know what to do except hang on.

When the buzzer sounded, Jack flung off hard; he hit the ground, jumped up out of the way of the whirling bull. Cricket leaped to her feet, her hands clasped, as everyone in the arena clapped wildly—when the announcer called out Jack's score of ninety-three and a half, the applause was earsplitting.

"We thought we saw you down here," Pete said, startling her.

"Did you see that?" Cricket cried, throwing her arms around Pete's neck.

"Yeah," he said, chuckling, "he's about to give Pop a coronary. Come sit up here with the family."

She scurried up after him, and hugged all the Morgans one by one. "Aren't you proud?" she asked Josiah, who wiped his brow.

"I'm just glad to be here," he said, "durn glad I am."

"Me, too," Cricket said. "*Me, too.*"

JACK LEANED his head against the boards of a stall, held his breath against the pain. *I can do this. I'm so close. I win, I have college education funds paid for, I can stay at home with my children the way my father never could. I can figure out a business that I can run from a tea shop. I can be with Cricket for as long as she'll put up with me.*

He'd read his mother's letters and he knew family was everything. Family was his dream. That's why he rode.

"Bro," Jack heard.

He raised his head. "Hey, Pete. What are you doing here?"

"Same thing we were doing here yesterday. Pop wanted to see you ride."

Jack perked up. "He did?"

"Oh, yeah. Wild horses couldn't have kept him away. Let's take a look at that knee." Pete squatted next to him. How Pete had found him, Jack wasn't sure. He'd found the most private place he could find to rest, hide, disguise the fact that his knee was killing him. He didn't want anyone telling him he couldn't ride.

"What do you mean, my knee?" Jack asked.

Pete shrugged. "You got a couple hours before you ride. There's a place down the street where we can put you in a bathtub and ice your knee."

Jack knew Pete's suggestion was wise. He still chafed at it, cursed his injury. "I'd really rather stay here."

Pete looked at him sideways. "Ice bath and a shot at a million, or pride and a knee that won't let you stay on."

"Have you seen the draw?" Jack asked.

"Man-O'-War," Pete said, needing no further elaboration.

A registered bounty bull. He was in a great place for the ride of his life—or the stomping of his life. "Ice," he said, "and an ibuprofen Big Gulp, durn it."

"Durn it" was Pop's favorite expression. Pete grinned.

"Now you're talking like a champ," Pete said, helping his brother up.

Actually he was *thinking* like Pop, Jack realized. Jack felt Pop's steely stubbornness strengthening him, and he was thankful.

CRICKET CALLED her family to check on the babies, reassured by her parents' calm words.

"Don't worry, Cricket," Eileen said, "I've raised a few children, you know. Anyway, we're delighted to have them all to ourselves. Three of them, three of us—we're equally matched, I'd say."

Cricket smiled. "Thank you."

"So, I'm almost too excited to ask, but how is Jack doing?"

"Fine, as far as I can tell," Cricket said. "He had a great ride this morning."

"Good," Eileen said. "Tell him we said 'bust a move' or whatever young people say these days. I heard that on TV. We've been watching kids' shows when we're feeding the children. Reed and I have decided we're going to order them some good old-fashioned sitcoms, like *The Honeymooners.* These kids aren't going to know about some of the best things in life if they have to grow up on what serves for family programming today."

Cricket smiled at the thought of her mother and father perusing old TV-show catalogs for her babies. "Thanks, Mom."

Eileen giggled. "You should see your father kowtow to these babies," she said on a whisper. "They don't wave a finger that he's not completely immersed in the moment."

202

"I'll call you later, Mom," Cricket said. "I hear the announcer saying something and I don't to miss anything."

"Good luck!" Eileen said, hanging up.

Cricket hurried back to her seat. "Did I miss anything?" She glanced around. "Where's Pete?"

"He went to do something," Gabe said. He handed her a bag of popcorn. "He should be back soon."

Cricket turned around, scanned the arena. Clowns moved barrels, workers began to take their positions where there were either open gates for departing bulls or help cowboys out of the arena. Cricket put the popcorn on the seat, suddenly lacking appetite. She whipped back around, staring at Dane and Gabe. "Pete went to see Jack, didn't he?"

"I believe so," Dane said, his voice calm.

Cricket realized he was trying to comfort her. "Because of his knee?"

"Because everybody needs a coach," Gabe said. "Don't worry, Cricket. Jack's ridden a ton of times, he's good at what he does."

"Okay." Cricket turned around, determined not to be the kind of woman who made everybody worry about her. Gisella briefly patted her on the back; Sara came and sat next to her. She took a deep breath, warmed by the support.

Before she realized it, the first bull of this round shot from the gate, accompanied by the announcer's voice excitedly calling his name. Cricket didn't hear a thing; it all blocked out. She heard Gabe say that Jack would ride last and consigned herself to sitting in a stonelike trance.

But this day wasn't about her, Cricket remembered, so silently she reached her hand over to Josiah, slipping her fingers between his. He didn't look at her, kept his gaze locked onto the arena, but he held her hand tightly.

"Jack Morgan!" the announcer called suddenly, "in second place, and needing a score of ninety-four to win! Ride, Man-O'-War, *Go-o-o-o-o-o*!"

Cricket and Josiah clutched each other's fingers; Pete, Gabe and Dane jumped to their feet. Gisella and Sara clung to each other as the bull threw itself in the air time and again, Jack hanging on with every ounce of his strength. Cricket could feel him straining; understood exactly what he was riding for, could even feel his focus. She'd never felt so close to him, almost reading his soul. In a flash, he went by, punishing leaps from the bull absorbed into his body. Cricket had no breath; she almost thought she saw a vision of three knights riding beside him, part of him, glorying in his quest.

The buzzer buzzed and with one mighty leap, the bull threw off Jack. He landed on the ground and Cricket was so dizzy she thought she saw the three knights help him to his feet. She and Josiah and all the family jumped up, cheering wildly.

"Did you see that, folks?" the announcer shouted with glee. "A bounty ride! A quicker-picker-upper if we ever saw one! Mighty Jack Morgan, folks, with a score of…ninety-five and a half! We have a winner of the Lonely Hearts Station Rodeo! Jumping Jack Flash!"

Someone shoved a microphone in front of Jack's face

as he rose from the ground. "Words from the winner!" the reporter demanded, and Jack took the microphone.

His chest was heaving, his face stuck with bits of sawdust, but he was grinning. "I do have something I want to say. I want to thank my sponsor, Lonely Hearts Station Rodeo, my family, the good Lord and his angels. But more than anything, I want to say to Cricket Jasper, deacon from Fort Wylie and the most amazing woman I have ever had the pleasure to meet—" he dropped onto his good knee "—Cricket Jasper, I love you like crazy, I'm in love with you the way I never thought I'd love anyone. To paraphrase an old movie, *The Music Man,* somewhere along the line I got my foot stuck on my way out the door when I met you. It's been the best thing that ever happened to me. Do me the honor of marrying me and I promise I'll be the husband you deserve."

The audience went wild, applauding and whistling. Cricket shot to her feet, but Jack didn't know where she was in the audience. She was blocked by cheering spectators.

Suddenly she felt lifted by strong hands, nearly helping her off her feet to the rail. She climbed over to rush across the sawdust-covered arena into Jack's arms. "I love you," she told him. "Of course I'll marry you. You're the prince I always dreamed of, my rodeo man."

He kissed her and the audience clapped louder, loving a happy ending and a good show, and Jack looked down at his deacon, then waved his cowboy hat to his family cheering in the stands.

Epilogue

Josiah loved having all his family around. Gisella adored living at the ranch, where it was always active, always filled with love. It was family, the way the Morgans had always dreamed it would be.

Jack turned, smiling at the huge ranch house he'd never thought he'd call home, where he now found sanctuary and peace. He went inside and found his wife in the den, putting the babies down for naps in the bassinets in front of the huge new windows she'd had installed. Streaming sun illuminated the room, which looked very much like a photograph straight out of *Southern Living*. The drapes Cricket had created were full, elegant swaths of rich fabric, framing the windows with perfect grace.

Cricket said she loved living in Union Junction, loved the Morgan ranch. Their lives had changed when Jack won the rodeo, but it had nothing to do with the money and everything to do with Jack's delight with being a father. He and Cricket had married in a lovely ceremony at the ranch. She'd taken a position as a deacon at a church in Union Junction, thrilled to be doing what she was good at once again. Her parents took over the tea shop, along with Thad, and they were enjoying their new position in the community. They spent a great deal of time running out to see the babies, who seemed to grow by leaps and bounds, and who never lacked loving arms to hold them and adoring hands to guide them. Jack bought Cricket the minivan he'd promised her, but his favorite gift was a three-stone engagement ring, one diamond for each baby she'd blessed him with.

Josiah gave his son the promised million dollars, which Jack decided to put toward his real dream of endowing a community college in Union Junction. Many times he'd pondered what Cricket had told Josiah that day in the hospital, when she'd told his father Jack was a huge believer in education. The thought had turned into a dream for children of Union Junction to have a college where they could expand their educations without leaving the town, if they wished. Pete, Dane and Gabe helped fund the college, and Josiah was chest-pounding proud. As far as building worlds went, he thought Jack had gotten the hang of it very well.

Cricket never did parachute again—she said one of them living dangerously was more than enough—but Jack did. He took Gisella up, with Thad's guidance. The experience was crazy, Gisella and Jack agreed, and it reconstructed a cherished bond that they had both always missed.

Jack admired his wife's handiwork for a few more moments, knowing how pleased his father would be with Cricket's choice of drapes, then gathered his wife into his arms and whispered something to her, soft words not even the babies could have heard.

But Cricket heard every word her husband spoke to her. She smiled at her rodeo man, and kissed him. "It's good to be home," Cricket said, and Jack nodded.

It had been said before, but there really was no place like home—and Jack's home was with Cricket and his triplets.

The true grail for the Morgans had been family.

* * * * *

June 2009 is a month to celebrate in Harlequin American Romance! In honor of Harlequin's 60th Anniversary, we're offering four special books by four special authors, including Tina Leonard's THE TEXAS TWINS, which features two stories— THE BILLIONAIRE AND THE BULL RIDER—in one!

Celebrate 60 years of pure reading pleasure with Harlequin®!
Silhouette® Romantic Suspense is celebrating with the glamour-filled, adrenaline-charged series LOVE IN 60 SECONDS *starting in April 2009.*
Six stories that promise to bring the glitz of Las Vegas, the danger of revenge, the mystery of a missing diamond, family scandals and ripped-from-the-headlines intrigue. Get your heart racing as love happens in sixty seconds!

Enjoy a sneak peek of USA TODAY *bestselling author Marie Ferrarella's* THE HEIRESS'S 2-WEEK AFFAIR *Available April 2009 from Silhouette® Romantic Suspense.*

Eight years ago Matt Shaffer had vanished out of Natalie Rothchild's life, leaving behind a one-line note tucked under a pillow that had grown cold: *I'm sorry, but this just isn't going to work.*

That was it. No explanation, no real indication of remorse. The note had been as clinical and compassionless as an eviction notice, which, in effect, it had been, Natalie thought as she navigated through the morning traffic. Matt had written the note to evict her from his life.

She'd spent the next two weeks crying, breaking down without warning as she walked down the street, or as she sat staring at a meal she couldn't bring herself to eat.

Candace, she remembered with a bittersweet pang, had tried to get her to go clubbing in order to get her to forget about Matt.

She'd turned her twin down, but she did get her act together. If Matt didn't think enough of their relationship to try to contact her, to try to make her understand why he'd changed so radically from lover to stranger, then to hell with him. He was dead to her, she resolved. And he'd remained that way.

Until twenty minutes ago.

The adrenaline in her veins kept mounting.

Natalie focused on her driving. Vegas in the daylight wasn't nearly as alluring, as magical and glitzy as it was after dark. Like an aging woman best seen in soft lighting, Vegas's imperfections were all visible in the daylight. Natalie supposed that was why people like her sister didn't like to get up until noon. They lived for the night.

Except that Candace could no longer do that.

The thought brought a fresh, sharp ache with it.

"Damn it, Candy, what a waste," Natalie murmured under her breath.

She pulled up before the Janus casino. One of the three valets currently on duty came to life and made a beeline for her vehicle.

"Welcome to the Janus," the young attendant said cheerfully as he opened her door with a flourish.

"We'll see," she replied solemnly.

As he pulled away with her car, Natalie looked up at the casino's logo. Janus was the Roman god with two faces, one pointed toward the past, the other facing the future. It struck her as rather ironic, given what she was doing here, seeking out someone from her past in order to get answers so that the future could be settled.

The moment she entered the casino, the Vegas phenomena took hold. It was like stepping into a world where time did not matter or even make an appearance. There was only a sense of "now."

Because in Natalie's experience she'd discovered that bartenders knew the inner workings of any establishment they worked for better than anyone else, she made her way to the first bar she saw within the casino.

The bartender in attendance was a gregarious man in his early forties. He had a quick, sexy smile, which was probably one of the main reasons he'd been hired. His name tag identified him as Kevin.

Moving to her end of the bar, Kevin asked, "What'll it be, pretty lady?"

"Information." She saw a dubious look cross his brow. To counter that, she took out her badge. Granted she wasn't here in an official capacity, but Kevin didn't need to know that. "Were you on duty last night?"

Kevin began to wipe the gleaming black surface of the bar. "You mean during the gala?"

"Yes."

The smile gracing his lips was a satisfied one. Last night had obviously been profitable for him, she judged. "I caught an extra shift."

She took out Candace's photograph and carefully placed it on the bar. "Did you happen to see this woman there?"

The bartender glanced at the picture. Mild interest turned to recognition. "You mean Candace Rothchild? Yeah, she was here, loud and brassy as always. But not for long," he added, looking rather disappointed. There was always a circus when Candace was around, Natalie thought. "She and the boss had at it and then he had our head of security escort her out."

She latched on to the first part of his statement. "They argued? About what?"

He shook his head. "Couldn't tell you. Too far away for anything but body language," he confessed.

"And the head of security?" she asked.

"He got her to leave."

She leaned in over the bar. "Tell me about him."

"Don't know much," the bartender admitted. "Just that his name's Matt Shaffer. Boss flew him in from L.A., where he was head of security for Montgomery Enterprises."

There was no avoiding it, she thought darkly. She was going to have to talk to Matt. The thought left her cold. "Do you know where I can find him right now?"

Kevin glanced at his watch. "He should be in his office. On the second floor, toward the rear." He gave her the numbers of the rooms where the monitors that kept watch over the casino guests as they tried their luck against the house were located.

Taking out a twenty, she placed it on the bar. "Thanks for your help."

Kevin slipped the bill into his vest pocket. "Any time, lovely lady," he called after her. "Any time."

She debated going up the stairs, then decided on the elevator. The car that took her up to the second floor was empty. Natalie stepped out of the elevator, looked around to get her bearings and then walked toward the rear of the floor.

"Into the Valley of Death rode the six hundred," she silently recited, digging deep for a line from a poem by

Tennyson. Wrapping her hand around a brass handle, she opened one of the glass doors and walked in.

The woman whose desk was closest to the door looked up. "You can't come in here. This is a restricted area."

Natalie already had her ID in her hand and held it up. "I'm looking for Matt Shaffer," she told the woman.

God, even saying his name made her mouth go dry. She was supposed to be over him, to have moved on with her life. What happened?

The woman began to answer her. "He's—"

"Right here."

The deep voice came from behind her. Natalie felt every single nerve ending go on tactical alert at the same moment that all the hairs at the back of her neck stood up. Eight years had passed, but she would have recognized his voice anywhere.

* * * * *

Why did Matt Shaffer leave heiress-turned-cop
Natalie Rothchild?
What does he know about the death of Natalie's
twin sister?
Come and meet these two reunited lovers and learn
the secrets of the Rothchild family in
THE HEIRESS'S 2-WEEK AFFAIR
by USA TODAY bestselling author
Marie Ferrarella.
The first book in Silhouette® Romantic Suspense's
wildly romantic new continuity,
LOVE IN 60 SECONDS!
Available April 2009.

CELEBRATE 60 YEARS

OF PURE READING PLEASURE
WITH HARLEQUIN®!

Look for Silhouette® Romantic Suspense in April!

Love In 60 Seconds

Bright lights. Big city. Hearts in overdrive.

Silhouette® Romantic Suspense is celebrating Harlequin's 60th Anniversary with six stories that promise to bring readers the glitz of Las Vegas, the danger of revenge, the mystery of a missing diamond, and family scandals.

Look for the first title, *The Heiress's 2-Week Affair* by *USA TODAY* bestselling author Marie Ferrarella, on sale in April!

His 7-Day Fiancée by **Gail Barrett**	May
The 9-Month Bodyguard by **Cindy Dees**	June
Prince Charming for 1 Night by **Nina Bruhns**	July
Her 24-Hour Protector by **Loreth Anne White**	August
5 minutes to Marriage by **Carla Cassidy**	September

You're invited to join our Tell Harlequin Reader Panel!

By joining our new reader panel you will:

- Receive Harlequin® books—they are FREE and yours to keep with no obligation to purchase anything!
- Participate in fun online surveys
- Exchange opinions and ideas with women just like you
- Have a say in our new book ideas and help us publish the best in women's fiction

In addition, you will have a chance to win great prizes and receive special gifts! See Web site for details. Some conditions apply. Space is limited.

To join, visit us at
www.TellHarlequin.com.

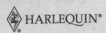
HARLEQUIN®

INTRIGUE

B.J. DANIELS

FIVE BROTHERS

ONE MARRIAGE-PACT
RACE TO THE HITCHING POST

WHITEHORSE
MONTANA
The Corbetts

SHOTGUN BRIDE

Available April 2009

Catch all five adventures in
this new exciting miniseries
from B.J. Daniels!

HI69392

REQUEST YOUR FREE BOOKS!

2 FREE NOVELS PLUS 2
FREE GIFTS!

Love, Home & Happiness!

YES! Please send me 2 FREE Harlequin® American Romance® novels and my 2 FREE gifts (gifts are worth about $10). After receiving them, if I don't wish to receive any more books, I can return the shipping statement marked "cancel." If I don't cancel, I will receive 4 brand-new novels every month and be billed just $4.24 per book in the U.S. or $4.99 per book in Canada. That's a savings of close to 15% off the cover price! It's quite a bargain! Shipping and handling is just 25¢ per book, along with any applicable taxes.* I understand that accepting the 2 free books and gifts places me under no obligation to buy anything. I can always return a shipment and cancel at any time. Even if I never buy another book from Harlequin, the two free books and gifts are mine to keep forever.

154 HDN EEZK 354 HDN EEZV

Name	(PLEASE PRINT)
Address	Apt. #
City	State/Prov.	Zip/Postal Code

Signature (if under 18, a parent or guardian must sign)

Mail to the Harlequin Reader Service:
IN U.S.A.: P.O. Box 1867, Buffalo, NY 14240-1867
IN CANADA: P.O. Box 609, Fort Erie, Ontario L2A 5X3

Not valid to current subscribers of Harlequin® American Romance® books.

Want to try two free books from another line?
Call 1-800-873-8635 or visit www.morefreebooks.com.

* Terms and prices subject to change without notice. N.Y. residents add applicable sales tax. Canadian residents will be charged applicable provincial taxes and GST. Offer not valid in Quebec. This offer is limited to one order per household. All orders subject to approval. Credit or debit balances in a customer's account(s) may be offset by any other outstanding balance owed by or to the customer. Please allow 4 to 6 weeks for delivery. Offer available while quantities last.

Your Privacy: Harlequin is committed to protecting your privacy. Our Privacy Policy is available online at www.eHarlequin.com or upon request from the Reader Service. From time to time we make our lists of customers available to reputable third parties who may have a product or service of interest to you. If you would prefer we not share your name and address, please check here. ☐

HAR08R2